Curtain of Control

Shubh Mehta

To Hill Spring International School, where dreams take flight and curiosity finds wings - thank you for nurturing not just my mind, but my imagination.

To my teachers, who saw potential in my endless questions and encouraged me to seek answers beyond textbooks - your guidance has shaped more than just my education.

To my friends, for always cheering me on when I've had a bad writing day, and for always unblocking my writer's block

And most importantly, to my parents, whose unwavering support has been my foundation and my strength. Your sacrifices have been my stepping stones, your encouragement my guiding star, and your love my greatest inspiration. Every word on these pages exists because you believed in me even when I didn't believe in myself.

For the late-night cups of milk during writing sessions, for listening to endless plot ideas, for understanding when I lived more in my fictional worlds than the real one - thank you will never be enough.

This book is for you, your love is the ink that writes my stories.

Prologue

15 years earlier

The sharp crack of gunfire echoed through the crisp mountain air as Sarah Rivera adjusted her ten-year-old son's stance, her hands steady on his shoulders. Mark flinched slightly at the recoil but maintained his grip on the .22 rifle just as his mother had taught him. The early morning sun cast long shadows across the makeshift range they'd set up on their remote Colorado property, the scent of gunpowder mingling with pine. "Remember, Mark," Sarah said, her voice carrying the same precision she brought to her work as a competitive shooter and firearms instructor, "a weapon is only as good as the conscience behind it. Power without principle is just violence."

Sarah's dark hair was pulled back in a practical braid, her keen eyes scanning the target downrange. She'd spent fifteen years in private security before transitioning to training, and she'd seen firsthand how power could corrupt. The memories of corporate corruption she'd witnessed during her time protecting tech executives still haunted her, driving her determination to prepare her son for the world's harsh realities. Nearby, David Rivera watched his wife and son with quiet pride. His muscular frame, honed by decades of martial arts training and military service, was relaxed but alert – a habit ingrained from years of special forces operations. The scars on his knuckles and the slight limp in his left leg told stories he'd never share with his family, classified missions that had shown him the darkness lurking beneath society's surface.

"Your mother's right," David called out, moving to join them at the range. "Everything we're teaching you – the shooting, the martial arts – it's not about fighting. It's about protecting those who can't protect themselves." Mark nodded solemnly, understanding even at his young age that his parents were preparing him for something more than just self-defense. He'd already begun learning Krav Maga from his father, the brutal efficiency of the martial art balanced by David's emphasis on discipline and restraint.

"Again," Sarah instructed, helping Mark reload the rifle. "This time, focus on your breathing. Remember what we talked about – slow inhale, gentle squeeze on the exhale." As Mark took aim at the target, Sarah caught David's eye. They shared a knowing look, both aware of the weight of their responsibility. They'd chosen this life – the remote property, the rigorous training, the careful preparation – because they'd seen too much to believe the world was safe.

Sarah's mind drifted to her last assignment in corporate security, the night she'd discovered documents that exposed widespread surveillance of private citizens. She'd brought her concerns to her superiors, only to find herself suddenly "redundant" and facing veiled threats. That experience had taught her the value of preparation, of having the skills to stand up against corruption. David stepped forward, placing his hand on Mark's shoulder as the boy squeezed off another round. The shot hit near the center of the target, drawing a small smile from both parents. "Good," David said. "Now, let's work on your speed without sacrificing accuracy." The morning progressed with a familiar rhythm – shooting drills interspersed with martial arts practice. David led Mark through a series of Krav Maga combinations, his movements fluid despite his old injuries. He'd learned these techniques in the military, refined them through years of private training, and now passed them on to his son with the hope that Mark would never need to use them.

"The world is changing," David explained as he demonstrated a defensive maneuver. "Technology is advancing faster than our ability to control it. People with power are using that technology to gain more power, to control those who don't understand the threats they face." Mark absorbed his father's words, just as he absorbed every lesson. At ten, he was already showing an aptitude for both physical training and technical skills. Sarah had begun teaching him basic computer programming, recognizing that in the modern world, digital literacy was as important as marksmanship.

As the sun climbed higher in the sky, the family moved their training indoors. Their home, a modernized cabin set against the backdrop of the Rockies, housed a state-of-the-art computer setup alongside their training equipment. Sarah sat with Mark at the computer, guiding him through basic encryption techniques while David prepared lunch.

"Knowledge is power," Sarah said, watching Mark's fingers move across the keyboard. "But remember, with power comes responsibility.

Everything we're teaching you – the physical skills, the technical knowledge – it's all meant to protect, never to harm." The afternoon brought more training: advanced first aid, survival skills, and situational awareness exercises. By evening, Mark was exhausted but satisfied, his young mind processing the day's lessons as he sat with his parents on their back deck, watching the sunset paint the mountains in shades of gold and purple.

"Mom," Mark asked, breaking the comfortable silence, "why did you leave your old job? The one in corporate security?" Sarah exchanged a glance with David before answering. "Sometimes, Mark, you discover things that powerful people want to keep hidden. When that happens, you have to make a choice – stay quiet and safe, or stand up for what's right."

"And you stood up?" Mark asked, though he already knew the answer. "We both did," David replied, his voice carrying the weight of memory. "That's why we're here now, why we're teaching you these skills. Because sometimes standing up for what's right comes at a price."

The conversation was interrupted by a distant rumble of thunder. As storm clouds gathered over the mountains, the family moved inside, securing their equipment and preparing for the night. Mark helped his father check the property's security systems while Sarah monitored their encrypted communications channels – another habit from their previous lives.

Later that night, as Mark slept, Sarah and David sat in their small home office, discussing their son's progress and the future they feared he might face. "He's learning quickly," Sarah observed, reviewing the day's training logs. "Faster than I expected."

David nodded, his expression thoughtful. "He'll need to. The world isn't getting any safer. The things we saw, the corruption we exposed – it's only gotten worse. More sophisticated, more deeply embedded in the system."Do you ever regret it?" Sarah asked softly. "Leaving our old lives behind, choosing this path?"

David reached for his wife's hand, his calloused fingers intertwining with hers. "Never. We're giving Mark the tools he needs to survive, to fight back if necessary. And maybe, just maybe, to succeed where we failed." Outside, the storm broke over the mountains, lightning illuminating the landscape in brief, brilliant flashes. Inside their fortress of preparation and principle, the Rivera family slept soundly, unaware that the skills they were cultivating would one day be tested in ways they could never have imagined. The lessons continued through the years, each building upon the last. Mark grew stronger, faster, more skilled in both physical combat and digital warfare. His parents' teachings became instinct, their principles woven into the fabric of his character.

Sarah and David Rivera were brutally murdered
in a police encounter just five years later.

1

The city's heart pulsed with a relentless rhythm as the sun dipped below the horizon, casting an eerie glow across the towering skyscrapers that dominated the skyline. Amidst the bustling streets and the cacophony of urban life, Mark Rivera found solace in the quiet confines of his office at TechNova, the leading technology firm that had taken the world by storm.

Mark leaned back in his chair, his eyes fixed on the lines of code that danced across his computer screen. The soft hum of the servers and the gentle tapping of his keyboard were the only sounds that broke the stillness of the empty office. As a senior software engineer, Mark was accustomed to working late hours, driven by an insatiable thirst for innovation and a relentless pursuit of perfection.

He paused for a moment, rubbing his tired eyes before reaching for the steaming mug of coffee that sat beside his keyboard. The bitter liquid jolted him awake, and he relished the warmth that spread through his body. Mark glanced at the clock on the wall, its hands inching towards midnight. He knew he should call it a night, but the allure of solving the complex problem that had been plaguing him for days was too strong to resist.

The code on his screen blurred as his mind drifted to the changes he'd noticed at TechNova over the past few months. Small things at first – new security measures, restricted access to certain floors, closed-door meetings that left executives looking troubled. He'd dismissed his concerns, telling himself it was natural for a rapidly growing tech company to implement tighter controls. Now, though, those small changes had begun to form a pattern he couldn't quite decipher.

Mark had always prided himself on his integrity and unwavering commitment to doing what was right. He had joined TechNova with the belief that technology could be a force for good, a tool to empower people and create a better world. But lately, he had begun to question the motives behind the company's actions and the true nature of its leadership.

A ring cut through the eerie silence of the office, it was unpleasantly, unusually loud. He glanced at the screen, surprised to see his sister's name flashing urgently. With a sense of unease, he answered the call.

"Emily? What's up?" Mark asked, trying to keep his tone light despite the knot forming in his stomach.

"Mark, listen to me," Emily's voice was strained, barely audible over the chaos in the background. "You need to be careful. They're coming for you."

Mark's heart raced as he processed her words. "What? Who's coming for me? Emily, what's going on?"

"I don't have much time," Emily panted, her breathing labored. "They broke into my apartment. I tried to fight them off, but there were too many."

The sound of shattering glass and splintering wood filled Mark's ear, followed by a pained cry from Emily. Mark's grip tightened on the phone, his knuckles turning white.

"Emily! Are you okay? Talk to me!" Mark pleaded, his voice rising with panic.

"I'm hurt, Mark," Emily gasped, her voice growing weaker. "They... they stabbed me. I'm losing a lot of blood."

Mark's world tilted on its axis. His sister, his confidante, his rock, was in danger, and he was miles away, helpless. "Emily, hang on. I'm coming to get you. Just stay with me, okay?"

"No, Mark, you can't!" Emily's voice was desperate. "They're looking for you too. It's not safe. You need to hide."

"I'm not leaving you," Mark declared, his jaw clenched with determination. "I'll find a way to get to you. Just hold on, Emily. Please."

"Mark, listen to me," Emily's voice was fading, the urgency in her tone palpable. "It's TechNova. They're behind this. They found out about my investigation. You need to be careful. Trust no one."

Mark's mind reeled with the revelation. TechNova, the company he had dedicated years of his life to, was somehow involved in an attack on his sister. The betrayal cut deep, fueling his anger and resolve.

"I'll find out who did this, Emily," Mark promised, his voice steely. "I won't let them get away with it."

"I know you won't," Emily whispered, her words barely audible. "I love you, Mark. Be safe."

The line went dead, leaving Mark in a suffocating silence. He stood frozen, the phone still pressed to his ear, with his dad's mantra echoing in his head 'Fear is the mind's way of identifying threats. Listen to it, don't let it control you'.

It then hit him, his sister, his only family, was fighting for her life, and he had no idea who he could trust. Emily had always been the level-headed one, the voice of reason in their family, the Emily he knew would be laughing after being stabbed, but the panic in her voice sent chills down Mark's spine, his instincts kicked into overdrive as he quickly saved his work and shut down his computer. He grabbed his jacket and headed towards the door, his heart racing with every step. As he stepped out into the dimly lit corridor, he couldn't shake the feeling that he was being watched.

The empty hallways of TechNova's headquarters seemed to stretch on forever as Mark made his way towards the elevator. The silence was deafening, broken only by the sound of his own footsteps echoing off the polished marble floors. Mark's mind raced with a thousand questions, trying to make sense of Emily's warning and the dark secrets that lurked within the company he had once trusted.

As he reached the elevator, Mark hesitated, his finger hovering over the call button. Suddenly, a glint of metal caught his eye, and he whirled around just in time to see a shadowy figure emerge from the darkness, a gun aimed squarely at his chest.

Mark's heart leaped into his throat as he stared down the barrel of the gun, his body paralyzed with fear. The figure stepped closer, their face obscured by a dark hood pulled low over their brow. The air crackled with tension as Mark found himself face to face with an unknown assailant, his life hanging in the balance.

"You should have stayed out of it, Rivera," the figure growled, their voice distorted by a modulator. "You have no idea what you're up against."

Mark's mind raced as he tried to find a way out of the deadly situation. He had never been one for confrontation, preferring to solve problems with his intellect rather than his fists, even after being extensively trained. But now, with a gun pointed at his chest and his sister's warning ringing in his ears, he knew he had no choice but to fight.

In a split second, Mark lunged to the side, narrowly avoiding the bullet that tore through the air where he had been standing moments before. The gunshot echoed through the empty hallway, shattering the eerie silence. Mark scrambled to his feet, his heart pounding in his ears as he raced towards the stairwell, desperately seeking an escape route, even under pressure, his mom's wise words coming to him, "The best defence isn't a good offence - it's not being there when they attack.". He saw the emergency exit, wide open, almost inviting, and he set off.

The assailant gave chase, his footsteps pounding behind him as Mark burst through the door and began descending the stairs two at a time. His lungs burned with every breath, and his muscles screamed in protest, but he pushed himself forward, driven by the primal instinct to survive.

Gunshots rang out behind him, the bullets ricocheting off the concrete walls in a deadly symphony. Mark ducked and weaved, his movements fueled by adrenaline and desperation. He could feel the hot breath of his pursuer on the back of his neck, their presence looming ever closer as he raced down the seemingly endless flights of stairs.

As he reached the ground floor, Mark burst through the emergency exit, stumbling out into the cool night air. The city streets were eerily deserted, the usual bustle of activity replaced by an unsettling stillness. Mark glanced over his shoulder, his heart hammering in his chest as he saw the assailant emerge from the building, their gun still trained on him.

With no time to lose, Mark sprinted down the street, his feet pounding against the pavement as he zigzagged through the maze of buildings. The sound of gunfire echoed behind him, spurring him on as he pushed himself to the limits of his endurance.

Mark's mind raced as he tried to make sense of the chaos that had engulfed his life in a matter of moments. His sister's warning, the mysterious assailant, and the dark secrets lurking within TechNova all swirled together in a dizzying kaleidoscope of confusion and fear.

As he rounded a corner, Mark's foot caught on an uneven piece of pavement, sending him sprawling to the ground. Pain shot through his body as he hit the concrete, his vision blurring from the impact. He struggled to push himself back up, his limbs shaking with exhaustion and terror.

The sound of approaching footsteps sent a jolt of panic through Mark's veins. He scrambled to his feet, ignoring the searing pain in his ankle as he limped forward, desperately seeking shelter.

Just as he thought all hope was lost, Mark spotted a narrow alleyway tucked between two buildings. With a final burst of energy, he stumbled into the shadows, pressing himself against the cool brick wall as he tried to calm his ragged breathing.

The footsteps grew louder, and Mark held his

breath, his heart pounding so loudly he was sure it would give away his location. The seconds ticked by with agonizing slowness as he waited for the inevitable discovery, his mind racing with thoughts of his sister and the terrible fate that awaited them both.

But the footsteps passed by the alleyway, fading into the distance as the assailant continued their relentless pursuit. Mark let out a shaky breath, his body sagging against the wall in relief.

As he caught his breath, Mark's mind began to race with questions. What had Emily discovered about TechNova that had put their lives in danger? What dark secrets lay buried beneath the company's glossy veneer of success and innovation?

With renewed determination, Mark pushed himself off the wall, wincing as pain shot through his injured ankle. He limped out of the alleyway, his eyes darting in every direction as he scanned the streets for any sign of his pursuer.

The city that had once felt like home now

seemed alien and hostile, every shadow hiding a potential threat. Mark knew he couldn't trust anyone, not even his colleagues at TechNova. The only person he could rely on was himself.

As he made his way through the deserted streets, Mark's mind turned to Emily. He had to find her, to make sure she was safe. But first, he needed answers. He needed to unravel the web of lies and deceit that had entangled them both.

Mark's journey had only just begun, but he knew that the path ahead would be fraught with danger and uncertainty. With each step, he ventured deeper into the heart of a conspiracy that threatened to tear apart everything he held dear.

But Mark was determined to fight, to uncover the truth and bring those responsible to justice. No matter the odds, no matter the risks, he would not rest until he had exposed the dark underbelly of TechNova and the corrupt forces that pulled its strings.

As the city's skyline loomed above him, Mark set his jaw and pressed forward, ready to face whatever challenges lay ahead. The attack, had been only the beginning, a glimpse into the sinister world he had unwittingly stumbled into.

But Mark Rivera was no ordinary software engineer. He was a fighter, a seeker of truth, and a force to be reckoned with. And he would stop at nothing until the truth was revealed and justice was served.

The sterile scent of disinfectant hung heavy in the air as Mark sat by Emily's bedside, his eyes fixed on the rhythmic rise and fall of her chest. The steady beep of the heart monitor was the only sound that punctuated the silence of the hospital room. Mark's mind raced with a whirlwind of emotions—anger, fear, and a growing sense of determination to uncover the truth behind the attack on his sister.

As he reached out to gently brush a strand of hair from Emily's forehead, a soft knock on the door startled him from his thoughts. Mark turned to see a figure standing in the doorway, shrouded in the dim light of the hallway. The man was tall and lean, with sharp features and piercing blue eyes that seemed to bore into Mark's soul.

"Mark Rivera?" the man asked, his voice low and steady.

Mark stood up, his body tense and on guard. "Who are you?"

The man stepped into the room, closing the door behind him. "My name is Ethan. I have information about the attack on your sister and TechNova's involvement."

Mark's heart raced at the mention of TechNova. His sister had suspected the company's connection to the attack, but hearing it from a stranger only intensified his suspicions. "What do you know?" he demanded, his voice trembling with a mix of fear and anger.

Ethan moved closer, his eyes darting around the room as if checking for hidden cameras or listening devices. "TechNova's enforcers are responsible for the attack on your sister. They see her as a threat, and they won't stop until they silence anyone who stands in their way."

Mark's hands clenched into fists at his sides and the beeping in the room got a lot faster, Emily was in an induced coma, but she too could hear and comprehend this, she too knew it was TechNova and she didn't need control over her voice to convey that.

The thought of TechNova deliberately targeting Emily filled Mark with a rage he had never experienced before. "Why are you telling me this?" he asked, his voice strained.

Ethan's expression remained stoic, but there was a flicker of something in his eyes—a hint of empathy, perhaps. "Because I want to help you uncover the truth. I have my own reasons for wanting to take down TechNova, but I can't do it alone."

Mark's mind raced with questions and doubts. Could he trust this stranger? What if Ethan was just another pawn in TechNova's game, sent to lure him into a trap? But the desperation to find answers and the burning desire for justice pushed him forward.

"What do you propose?" Mark asked, his voice cautious but determined.

Ethan reached into his pocket and pulled out a small, plain white business card. "Meet me at this address tomorrow at noon. Come alone. I'll provide you with the evidence you need to expose TechNova's crimes."

Mark hesitated for a moment before taking the card, his fingers brushing against Ethan's as he did so. The touch sent a shiver down his spine, a reminder of the dangerous path he was about to embark upon.

As Ethan turned to leave, Mark called out after him. "Wait! How do I know I can trust you?"

Ethan paused, his hand on the doorknob. He looked back at Mark, his blue eyes intense and unwavering. "You don't. But right now, I'm the only ally you've got."

With that, Ethan disappeared into the hallway, leaving Mark alone with his thoughts and the weight of the decision before him. He looked down at Emily, her face peaceful in the depths of her medically-induced slumber. The sight of her, so vulnerable and broken, strengthened his resolve.

Mark knew that trusting Ethan was a risk, but it was a risk he had to take. For Emily, for the truth, and for the chance to bring TechNova to justice. He tucked the business card into his pocket and settled back into the chair beside Emily's bed, his mind already racing with plans and possibilities.

As the hours ticked by, Mark's thoughts drifted to the people in his life—his parents, his co-workers, and his few close friends. He had always been a private person, keeping his personal life separate from his work at TechNova. But now, with the company's dark secrets threatening to unravel everything he held dear, he realized just how isolated he had become.

The weight of the responsibility he now carried settled heavily on his shoulders. Mark knew that the path ahead would be treacherous, filled with danger and uncertainty at every turn. But he also knew that he couldn't turn back now. Not when Emily's life hung in the balance, and the truth about TechNova's misdeeds remained hidden in the shadows.

As the first light of dawn began to filter through the hospital window, Mark's exhaustion finally caught up with him. He dozed off in the chair, his hand still clasping Emily's, as if he could somehow protect her from the dark forces that threatened to tear their lives apart.

When he awoke a few hours later, groggy and disoriented, Mark's first thought was of the meeting with Ethan. He checked his watch and realized he had just enough time to make it to the address on the card.

With a heavy heart, Mark leaned over and placed a gentle kiss on Emily's forehead. "I'll make this right, Em," he whispered, his voice hoarse with emotion. "I promise." At the mention of a promise, something twitched, Mark noticed it to be the pinky finger on Emily's right hand. 'Even through a coma huh' thought Mark to himself, as he wrapped his own pinky around hers, 'Pinky promise, Em'. Since he was 3 he'd never broken a pinky promise, and he definitely wasn't going to do it now.

As he stepped out of the hospital room and into the bright sunlight of the morning, Mark felt a renewed sense of purpose coursing through his veins. He didn't know what the future held, but he knew that he would stop at nothing to uncover the truth and bring TechNova to its knees.

With each step he took towards the unknown, Mark's resolve grew stronger. He was no longer just a software engineer, but a man on a mission. A man determined to fight for justice, no matter the cost.

As he hailed a taxi and climbed inside, Mark's mind raced with the possibilities of what lay ahead. The business card in his pocket seemed to burn with the promise of answers, and the weight of the secrets he carried threatened to consume him.

But Mark pushed forward, his jaw set with determination. He had made a promise to Emily, and he intended to keep it. No matter the danger, no matter the risk, he would unravel the web of deceit that surrounded TechNova and expose the truth to the world.

As the taxi sped through the city streets, Mark's thoughts turned to Ethan and the mysterious offer of help. He knew that trusting a stranger was a gamble, but in a world where the lines between friend and foe had become blurred, it was a gamble he had to take.

The city passed by in a blur of glass and steel, a reminder of the cold, unfeeling nature of the technology that had once been Mark's passion. But now, as he faced the darkest depths of the industry he had once revered, Mark realized that his true passion lay in the pursuit of justice and the defense of those he loved.

As the taxi pulled up to the address on the card, Mark took a deep breath, steeling himself for the unknown that lay ahead. With a final glance at the world he was leaving behind, he stepped out of the car and into the shadows, ready to face whatever challenges the future might bring.

The dimly lit alleyway reeked of stale cigarettes and rotting garbage as Mark cautiously made his way towards the designated meeting point. His heart pounded in his chest, echoing the rapid footsteps that reverberated off the damp, graffiti-covered walls. The weight of Emily's hospital room key in his pocket served as a constant reminder of the grave situation he found himself in.

Mark's mind raced with thoughts of his sister, Emily, lying in a hospital bed, her life hanging in the balance after the vicious attack orchestrated by TechNova's enforcers. The very thought of the powerful technology firm sent a shiver down his spine, knowing that he was about to embark on a dangerous journey to uncover the truth behind their sinister actions.

As he approached the end of the alleyway,

Mark's eyes darted nervously, searching for any signs of the whistleblower who had contacted him. The eerie silence was suddenly shattered by the sound of approaching footsteps, and Mark instinctively reached for the concealed weapon tucked beneath his jacket.

"Mark Rivera?" a voice called out from the shadows, causing Mark to whirl around, his heart skipping a beat.

A figure emerged from the darkness, hands raised in a non-threatening manner. It was Ethan, a former TechNova employee turned whistleblower, who had reached out to Mark with crucial information about the company's corrupt practices.

"I'm glad you came," Ethan said, his voice trembling slightly. "I wasn't sure if you would trust me."

Mark studied Ethan's face, searching for any signs of deception. The man's eyes were filled with a mixture of fear and determination, mirroring the emotions that swirled within Mark's own mind.

"I don't have much choice," Mark replied, his voice low and steady. "My sister's life is on the line, and I need answers."

Ethan nodded solemnly, glancing over his shoulder before speaking. "TechNova's influence runs deeper than you can imagine. They've infiltrated every level of government, and their enforcers are just the tip of the iceberg."

Mark felt a knot form in his stomach as Ethan's words sank in. The realization that he was up against a formidable force, one that held immense power and resources, was both daunting and infuriating.

"What evidence do you have?" Mark asked, his mind already racing with possibilities.

Ethan reached into his jacket and retrieved a small, nondescript envelope, within it a single, unmarked USB drive. "In here, you'll find documents that prove TechNova's involvement in illegal surveillance, data manipulation, and even human experimentation. It's just the beginning, but it's enough to start exposing their crimes."

As Mark reached for the envelope, a sudden commotion erupted from the entrance of the alleyway. The sound of screeching tires and shouting voices filled the air, causing both men to freeze in terror.

"They found me," Ethan whispered, his face draining of color. "You need to run, Mark. Don't let them catch you."

Mark's mind raced as he assessed the situation. He knew that if TechNova's enforcers caught him with the evidence, his life would be forfeit. But he also couldn't leave Ethan to face them alone.

In a split-second decision, Mark grabbed Ethan's arm and pulled him deeper into the alleyway, his eyes searching for an escape route. The sound of heavy footsteps and barking orders grew closer, and Mark's heart pounded in his ears.

"This way," he hissed, yanking Ethan towards a narrow side street.

As they ran, the weight of the evidence in Mark's pocket seemed to grow heavier with each step. He knew that the information contained within could bring TechNova to its knees, but the price of that knowledge was becoming increasingly clear.

Suddenly, a figure stepped out from the shadows, blocking their path. Mark skidded to a halt, his hand instinctively reaching for his weapon. The figure was dressed in a crisp suit, an air of authority emanating from his posture.

"Mark Rivera," the man said, his voice smooth and calculated. "I believe you have something that belongs to us."

Mark's eyes narrowed as he recognized the man as a high-ranking police official, he thought he'd seen him somewhere, but couldn't quite place where.

"I don't know what you're talking about," Mark replied, his voice steady despite the fear that gripped his heart.

The official smiled, a cold and predatory expression that sent shivers down Mark's spine. "Don't play games with me, Mr. Rivera. You have evidence that could be very damaging to certain interests. Hand it over, and we can make this all go away."

Mark's mind raced as he considered his options. He knew that the official's offer was a trap, a way to silence him and bury the truth forever. But he also knew that refusing would paint a target on his back, making him a hunted man in a city controlled by TechNova's influence.

Ethan's eyes widened in fear as he glanced between Mark and the official, his breath coming in short, panicked gasps.

"Mark, we need to get out of here," he whispered urgently.

Mark's jaw clenched as he made his decision. He couldn't let the evidence fall into the wrong hands, no matter the cost.

In a lightning-fast motion, Mark drew his weapon and aimed it at the official, his voice low and threatening. "Back off. I'm not giving you anything."

The official's eyes narrowed, a flicker of anger crossing his face. "You're making a grave mistake,

Mr. Rivera. You have no idea the forces you're dealing with."

Mark's finger tightened on the trigger, his heart pounding in his chest. He knew that this moment would define the rest of his life, that there was no turning back from the path he had chosen.

"I know enough," Mark replied, his voice filled with determination. "And I won't let you silence the truth."

The official's hand slowly reached for his own weapon, and Mark knew that he had only seconds to act. With a quick glance at Ethan, he made his move.

"Run!" Mark shouted, firing a warning shot that echoed through the alleyway.

Ethan didn't hesitate, sprinting down the side street as Mark provided cover fire. The official ducked for cover, shouting orders into a communication device as Mark and Ethan disappeared into the maze of alleyways.

As they ran, Mark's mind raced with the weight of the decision he had just made. He knew that he had just declared war on TechNova and the corrupt officials who protected them. His life would never be the same, and the danger that loomed ahead was unlike anything he had ever faced.

But as he clutched the evidence in his pocket, his phone rang, the letters sprung out of the screens and Mark's heart skipped a beat, 'Emily's nurse' it read. What could have happened to her, he couldn't lose her, not now. He picked up the phone, and crossed his fingers. "She has regained consciousness, and is responding normally" said the shrill voice on the other end, Mark's heart fluttered, as he said goodbye to Ethan and beelined it to the hospital. "Maybe everything will actually come back to normal, who knows"

2

The steady beep of hospital monitors filled the silence as Mark sat beside Emily's bed, his hand gentle around her bruised fingers. The past forty-eight hours felt like a nightmare - the phone call, the chase, finding his sister bleeding in her apartment. He'd been running on adrenaline and training, but now, in the sterile quiet of the hospital room, reality was crashing in.

"You should see your face right now," Emily's voice was weak but carried that familiar teasing tone. "Mom always said you had the worst poker face."

Mark tried to smile, but it didn't reach his eyes. "How are you feeling?"

"Like I got stabbed," Emily attempted a shrug, then winced. "But hey, at least I finally got to use those pain management techniques Dad taught us."

The attempt at humor fell flat as Mark studied his sister's pale face, taking in the dark circles under her eyes, the split lip, the bandages visible beneath her hospital gown. His free hand clenched into a fist.

"I'm going to TechNova," Mark said quietly. "I need answers."

Emily's grip on his hand tightened suddenly, surprising strength in her injured state. "Mark, no. You don't understand what you're dealing with. The things I found in their servers..." She broke off, coughing.

"Then help me understand," Mark leaned forward. "Tell me what you found."

Emily's eyes darted to the door, then the window, before meeting his gaze. "I can't. Not here. They're watching. But..." she squeezed his hand. "Remember Dad's old saying about digital footprints?"

Mark nodded slowly. "'Every keystroke leaves an echo.'"

"Check my gaming accounts," Emily whispered. "The ones we used to play on as kids. I left... breadcrumbs."

Her eyes were starting to droop, the pain medication taking hold. Mark stood, pressing a kiss to her forehead. "Rest. I'll figure this out."

"Mark?" Emily caught his hand, her voice barely audible. "Be careful. They're not what they seem. None of it is what it seems."

As Mark stepped into the hospital corridor, his parents' training kicked in. He noticed the security camera's slight tilt, the orderly who'd passed the room three times, the unmarked sedan in the parking lot visible from the window.

They were watching. Just like Emily said.

He pulled out his phone, hesitating over the keypad. He needed help, but who could he trust? The police? After what happened to Emily, he couldn't risk official channels. His coworkers? Any of them could be involved.

His father's voice echoed in his memory: "Sometimes the hardest battles are the ones you have to fight alone. Until you find the right allies."

Mark pocketed his phone. First, he needed to check Emily's gaming accounts, find those breadcrumbs she'd mentioned. Then he'd confront TechNova - not with accusations, but with questions. Watch their reactions. Gather intel.

Just like his parents taught him.

Because this wasn't about revenge. Not yet. First, he needed to understand what he was up against.

Looking back at Emily's room one last time, Mark set his jaw and headed for the exit. Whatever his sister had discovered, whatever TechNova was hiding, he would find out.

Back in his apartment, Mark booted up his old gaming PC. His hands moved automatically through Emily's favorite usernames - 'QuantumQueen', 'ByteStorm', 'NightOwl_Em'.

Each login attempt met with either expiration notices or password changes. Emily was too smart to leave anything that obvious.

Then he remembered their childhood coding games. Emily had always hidden messages in plain sight, using their parents' encryption methods. He pulled up her public gaming profiles, scanning through recent activity. There - in her Valorant stats. A series of matches with seemingly random scores, played at exact three-minute intervals.

"Clever, Em," he muttered, recognizing the pattern. Binary code disguised as game data.

Three hours and two pots of coffee later, Mark had his first real lead. Emily had embedded coordinates and a timestamp in her match history, pointing to a TechNova backup server facility. The same facility where she'd discovered... something. The files themselves weren't included, but her message was clear: the proof was there.

Mark checked his watch. 4:47 AM. In three hours, he was supposed to be at work, sitting at his desk at TechNova like nothing had changed. Like his sister hadn't been stabbed for discovering their secrets.

His mother's voice echoed in his memory: "Sometimes the best cover is routine. Let them think they've won."

He showered and dressed with mechanical precision, strapping on the concealed holster his mother had insisted he keep. The familiar weight of the gun brought both comfort and anxiety - he'd trained with it countless times, but had never needed to use it outside the range. Until two nights ago, when he'd faced that masked attacker in TechNova's hallway.

The morning commute felt surreal. Same traffic, same coffee shop crowd, same security guard nodding as he badged into TechNova's gleaming headquarters. But everything had changed. Every security camera felt malevolent, every colleague a potential threat.

Instead of heading to his usual floor, Mark took the elevator to the executive level. His senior developer credentials wouldn't get him into Maxwell Roth's office, but they'd get him close enough. Close enough to start finding answers.

"Mr. Rivera?" Roth's secretary looked up in surprise as Mark approached her desk. "Do you have an appointment?"

"No," Mark kept his voice steady, professional. "But I need to speak with Mr. Roth about my sister, Emily Rivera. He'll want to hear what I have to say."

The secretary's expression flickered - recognition, concern, and something else. Fear? She reached for her phone, but Mark was already moving past her desk.

"Sir, you can't-"

Mark pushed open the heavy oak doors to Roth's office. The CEO of TechNova looked up from his desk, Roth's office was a cathedral to corporate power - all glass, steel, and calculated intimidation. The CEO himself sat behind a massive desk of polished mahogany, deliberately engrossed in his tablet. Mark's footsteps echoed on the marble floor, each step feeling heavier than the last.

"Mr. Rivera," Roth didn't look up, his voice carrying the bored indifference of a man swatting a fly. "I suppose this is about your sister's... unfortunate accident?"

Mark's jaw clenched, muscles twitching beneath the skin. "We both know it wasn't an accident."

"Hmm." Roth finally looked up, studying Mark with the detached interest of a scientist observing a lab specimen. "You know, I've always found it fascinating how some people simply can't leave well enough alone. Your sister, for instance - such a promising journalist. Until she started asking the wrong questions."

The casual mention of Emily made Mark's hands curl into fists, knuckles white with strain. "What did she find?"

"Tell me, Mark," Roth set down his tablet, completely ignoring the question. "Did you ever wonder why your parents were so... paranoid? All those combat lessons, the survival training, the endless preparation for some nebulous threat?" A cold smile played at his lips. "Almost as if they knew something was coming for them."

The room seemed to tilt slightly, the morning light suddenly too harsh. Mark's throat went dry. "What are you talking about?"

Roth stood, moving to his window with deliberate slowness. "Your mother was quite the marksman, wasn't she? Sarah Rivera - top of her class in tactical shooting. And David, well... Special Forces training certainly gave him an edge. Until that tragic night five years ago."

Mark's pulse roared in his ears, his vision blurring at the edges. "The police report said-"

"Oh yes, the police report." Roth's voice dripped with mock sympathy. "A routine traffic stop gone wrong. Such a clean narrative. Simple. Believable." He turned, fixing Mark with a predator's stare. "Would you like to know what really happened?"

"Stop." The word came out as a whisper, Mark's chest tightening.

"They were getting close, you see. Too close. Just

like Emily. Must be genetic, this inability to mind your own business." Roth pressed a button on his desk. "Rodriguez, would you join us?"

The office door opened. Mark's world narrowed to a tunnel as TechNova's head of security entered - the man he'd passed in the lobby countless times, exchanged polite nods with, even shared elevator rides with. The man whose face he'd glimpsed in grainy police photos, standing over his parents' bodies.

"You remember Rodriguez, don't you?" Roth's voice seemed to come from far away. "He's been keeping an eye on you. Ever since that night."

Mark's legs weakened, his body swaying slightly. Bile rose in his throat as memories crashed over him - the late-night phone call, the morgue, the funeral where he'd held Emily as she sobbed. All while his parents' killer had been watching, waiting.

"Why?" The question scraped out of his raw throat.

"Because they were inconvenient." Roth's smile

widened, showing teeth. "Just like your sister became inconvenient. Though I must say, she proved surprisingly resilient. Rodriguez, how many times did she have to be stabbed before she stopped fighting?"

Something snapped inside Mark. With a roar that didn't sound human, he lunged for Roth. His vision went red, his body moving on pure instinct. But before he could reach the CEO, strong hands grabbed him from behind. Two security guards materialized, wrestling him to his knees.

"Look at him," Roth chuckled, straightening his tie. "All that training, all those years of preparation, and what good did it do? Your parents died bleeding on cold asphalt. Your sister lies in a hospital bed. And you?" He leaned down, close enough that Mark could smell his expensive cologne. "You're just a broken little boy playing at being a hero."

Mark thrashed against the guards' grip, tears streaming down his face, muscles straining until it felt like they would tear. "I'll kill you," he choked out between sobs. "I swear to God, I'll kill you."

"No, you won't." Roth's voice turned gentle, almost paternal, which somehow made it worse. "You'll walk out of here alive, because I want you to live with this. I want you to wake up every morning knowing that your parents' killer has been watching you. That we've been laughing at your pathetic attempts at a normal life. That everything you love can be taken away at our whim."

Rodriguez stepped forward, his face impassive. "Sir?"

"Show Mr. Rivera out. Gently. We wouldn't want another accident. Not yet." Roth returned to his desk. "Oh, and Mark? Those files your sister thought she hid so cleverly? We already have them. All of them. So don't bother looking."

The guards dragged Mark toward the door, his legs barely working, his chest heaving with ragged breaths. Tears and sweat mingled on his face, dripping onto the pristine marble floor.

"One last thing," Roth called out. "Your parents

spent years training you, didn't they? All those lessons, all that preparation. And yet..." his smile turned vicious, "here we are. All that training, and you couldn't save them. Just like you couldn't save Emily. Just like you can't save yourself."

The doors closed on Roth's soft laughter. In the elevator, Mark sagged between the guards, his body wracked with silent sobs. His shirt was soaked with sweat, his muscles trembling from exertion and shock. Rodriguez released him with a rough shove as they reached the lobby.

"The boss is being generous, letting you walk away," Rodriguez said quietly, a hint of cruel amusement in his voice. "Don't waste his mercy."

Mark stumbled out into the morning sunshine, his world in pieces. His legs gave out at the bottom of the steps, and he fell to his knees, retching. Passersby hurried past, avoiding the broken man whose anguished gasps echoed off the glass towers.

Mark looked up at TechNova's tower, tears still flowing, but something else building beneath the grief. Roth had wanted to break him with the truth. Instead, he'd given Mark something he'd lacked before.

Purpose.

His parents hadn't died by accident. Emily hadn't stumbled onto something random. This was all connected, and somewhere in his sister's digital breadcrumbs, there were allies waiting.

It was time to stop playing by the rules.

It was time to become what his parents had trained him to be.

3

Mark stared at his phone screen, the bright colors of Brawl Stars a stark contrast to his dark apartment. 3:47 AM. The game had become his lifeline these past few months - something about its simple chaos helping to quiet his mind. Tonight though, his hands trembled as he selected Edgar, his main since the day Emily had convinced him to download the game.

"The edgy parkour kid? Really, Sentinel?" Ghost's familiar teasing came through his earbuds. "Some things never change."

"Says the guy who only plays Crow," Mark managed, grateful for the attempt at normalcy. In their voice chat, he could hear the faint clicking of

Ghost's mechanical keyboard - always gaming on his custom PC, even for a mobile game.

"Crow is a strategic choice," Ghost defended. "Right, Wraith?"

"Don't drag me into your brawler debates." Wraith's dry tone carried its usual calm, but Mark caught the undertone of concern. She'd been watching his gameplay all night - the missed jumps, the reckless engages, the uncharacteristic silence between matches.

The game loaded - Gem Grab on Crystal Arcade. Ghost's Crow darted ahead immediately, scattering daggers. Wraith's Byron moved with surgical precision, supporting from the back. Mark's Edgar stood still at spawn, his fingers suddenly unable to move.

"Emily's in the hospital," he said abruptly. The words hung in the voice chat as his character took damage from a passing Colt. "TechNova... they tried to kill her."

The silence that followed was broken only by the game's cheerful background music, now feeling grotesquely inappropriate. Ghost's Crow retreated to their side of the map, abandoning the gems he'd collected. Wraith's Byron positioned himself between Mark's Edgar and the enemy team, buying him space.

"How bad?" Wraith asked, her voice carefully controlled.

"Multiple stab wounds. She's stable, but..." Mark's vision blurred, the game screen becoming a smear of colors. "I saw her today. My big sister, always so strong, always protecting me... she looked so small in that hospital bed."

"TechNova," Ghost's voice had lost all its playful edge. "Always with their 'accidents', aren't they? Always making examples of people who ask the wrong questions."

The match ended - they'd lost badly, none of them really playing. The post-game lobby loaded, but no one selected 'Play Again.'

"You ever wonder why I'm always online at these hours?" Ghost asked suddenly. The familiar sound of his keyboard had stopped. "Can't sleep in my own place anymore. Keep thinking I'll smell smoke. Keep hearing the screams..."

Mark's throat tightened. He'd heard the pain behind Ghost's jokes before, glimpsed the darkness beneath his cheerful gaming persona. "Ghost..."

"James," Ghost interrupted. "My real name is James Chen. I... I haven't told anyone that since the fire."

Another game loaded automatically - Bounty on Snake Prairie. The dark map felt fitting as Ghost's story poured out.

"Chen Electronics, in San Francisco's Chinatown. My parents' shop, but it was more than that. We helped low-income families get computers, taught kids to code. Mom and Dad came to America with nothing, built something beautiful..." His voice cracked. "I was their pride and joy - the tech prodigy who could make ATMs spit out cash with a modified Nintendo DS."

In the game, Ghost's Crow moved aggressively, almost recklessly, taking fights he'd normally avoid.

"I was fifteen when I found it - a backdoor in TechNova's code. They were using gaming platforms, social media, any digital space where kids gathered. Building profiles, flagging anyone who showed signs of being 'problematic' to their vision of the future. Independent thinking, questioning authority, even just being too good at strategy games... all marked for something called Project Harmony."

Mark's hands froze on his screen. Project Harmony. The same name Emily had mentioned in her fevered hospital ramblings.

"I thought I was being careful, covering my tracks. I was wrong." Ghost's laugh was hollow. "The fire looked like an electrical fault. Perfect accident. Sixteen people died. My parents. Three kids who were there for a coding workshop - Andy, Maria, and Kai. They were just... they were just kids who wanted to learn..."

The game continued in silence for a moment, their characters moving through the dark map like ghosts themselves. Mark noticed Ghost's gameplay becoming more erratic, more desperate - Crow diving into fights he couldn't win, as if seeking punishment.

"I was supposed to be there that day," Ghost continued, his voice barely a whisper. "Had a fever. Mom made me stay home, said I could teach the next coding class instead. I watched the shop burn from three blocks away. Couldn't... couldn't even scream. Just stood there, watching TechNova erase my whole world."

"Jesus, Ghost," Mark breathed. The game blurred as his eyes welled up.

"The worst part? They let me live. Left enough evidence of my hacking for me to know why it happened, but not enough to prove anything. Their message was clear: stay quiet, or more 'accidents' would happen."

"That's why you became Ghost," Wraith said softly. It wasn't a question.

"Yeah. Figured if I had to become a ghost, might as well haunt the bastards who killed my family."

His attempt at humor fell flat. "Been tracking TechNova ever since, watching them destroy more lives, waiting for a chance to..."

He trailed off as their match ended. In the lobby, Mark noticed Ghost switch from Crow to Edgar - his way of showing solidarity.

"Your turn, Wraith," Ghost said after a moment. "We're all sharing tragic backstories tonight, right?"

The silence stretched so long they thought she might have disconnected. Then: "They have my brother."

Her Byron remained selected, but her next words carried such weight that both Mark and Ghost felt their spines straighten.

"Dr. Alexandra Kane," she said, her clinical tone barely masking deep pain. "That was my name, before. Head of Neural Interface Research at TechNova's Advanced Technologies Division. I thought... I thought I was helping people."

A new match loaded - Siege on Factory Rush. The industrial setting seemed to trigger something in Wraith's memory.

"The neural interface was revolutionary. Designed to help trauma victims, PTSD patients, people trapped in their own minds. The ability to redirect neural pathways, modify behavioral patterns..." She paused as her Byron precisely eliminated an enemy. "I was so proud of my work. So blind to how it could be perverted."

"Project Harmony," Ghost said quietly.

"Yes." The word came out like a curse. "They took my research, my life's work, and turned it into... into something monstrous. Not just behavior modification. Complete cognitive control. The perfect tool for creating their compliant future."

Mark's Edgar stood still at spawn, his mind racing. His parents' training, Emily's discovery, Ghost's surveillance findings, Wraith's neural interface - pieces of a puzzle starting to form a terrifying picture.

"Thomas, my brother," Wraith continued, her voice growing tight. "He was a privacy advocate, led protests against corporate surveillance. When he discovered a connection between missing persons cases and TechNova, he came to warn me. I dismissed him. Told him he was being paranoid."

Her Byron moved with mechanical precision, but they could hear her breathing becoming uneven.

"A week later, he disappeared. I found his name in the Project Harmony test subject files. Subject 23-B. Not even his name anymore, just a number. When they... when they brought him back..."

Her voice broke completely. In the game, her character stopped moving, vulnerable in the open.

"He smiles when they want him to smile. Agrees with everything. Recites company propaganda like scripture. But his eyes... there's nothing behind them anymore. Sometimes though, just for a moment, I see him fighting. The real Thomas, trapped inside his own mind, screaming to get out."

"Can it be reversed?" Mark asked, thinking of Emily in her hospital bed, of how close TechNova had come to silencing her.

"I don't know," Wraith admitted. "They keep him in the program, living in a TechNova 'rehabilitation facility.' Every time I visit, every time I see what they've done to him... but I can't stop visiting. Can't stop hoping that one day I'll find a way to bring him back."

The match ended, but none of them noticed the defeat screen. The game had become just background noise, a thin veneer of normalcy over their shared trauma.

"I keep all his old things," Wraith continued, her voice distant. "His protest signs, his privacy rights papers, his laptop... I can't access it, of course. Thomas was paranoid about security, had everything encrypted. But I keep it all, hoping that when - not if, when - I get him back, he'll need those pieces of himself."

"Tell us about him," Ghost encouraged gently. "The real Thomas."

A new match loaded - Showdown on Forsaken Falls. The desolate map seemed appropriate.

"He was brilliant," Wraith's voice softened with memory. "Graduated MIT at nineteen, could have worked anywhere. But he chose to fight for privacy rights, for individual freedom. Used to tease me about working for 'the corporate overlords' at TechNova." A bitter laugh escaped her. "Guess he was right about them all along."

Mark's Edgar moved closer to Wraith's Byron in the game, providing cover as she continued.

"The last time I saw him - the real him - he was so excited. Said he'd found something big, a connection between TechNova and dozens of missing persons cases. Young people, mostly. Activists, hackers, anyone who posed a threat to their vision of 'social harmony.'"

"Like the kids they flagged through my gaming backdoor," Ghost added quietly.

"Exactly. Thomas had started mapping it all out - the surveillance network, the disappearances, the behavioral modifications. He came to my lab that night, trying one last time to make me see the truth." Her voice cracked. "I was so convinced he was just being paranoid. Told him to stop digging before he got himself into trouble."

"And then?" Mark prompted, though he feared he knew the answer.

"Three days later, my access card stopped working. Security escorted me from the building - 'routine restructuring,' they said. When I got home, Thomas was gone. His apartment looked like he'd just... vanished. Mid-sentence in his research notes, coffee still warm in the mug..."

Ghost's Crow moved to their position, forming a protective triangle in the game map's center.

"It took me two weeks to hack into Project Harmony's files," Wraith continued. "Found him listed as 'Subject 23-B: Successful Integration.' They..." her voice shook with rage and grief. "They documented everything. Every step of breaking him down, rewriting his neural pathways, turning my own research against my brother's mind."

"The first time they let me see him, he was sitting in a TechNova 'wellness center,' watching corporate propaganda videos with this empty smile. Didn't even recognize me at first. When he did, he just... recited their company values. Told me how happy he was to be 'part of the TechNova family.'"

Mark felt sick. He thought of Emily's warning, of Roth's smirking face: "Your parents knew something was coming for them."

"But sometimes," Wraith's voice dropped to a whisper, "sometimes I see him fighting it. Little things - a twitch when they mention privacy rights, a slight hesitation before reciting their mantras. Last month, just for a second, he grabbed my hand and his eyes... his real eyes were there, terrified, trying to tell me something. Then it was gone, replaced by that empty smile."

The game's storm circle closed in, forcing their characters closer together.

"I've been trying to reconstruct my research," she continued. "Find a way to reverse the neural modifications. But they were thorough - destroyed all my original work, buried the Project Harmony protocols behind layers of security. And every failed attempt, every dead end... that's another day Thomas stays trapped in there."

"We'll help you get him back," Ghost said firmly. "Right, Mark?"

Mark stared at his screen, seeing beyond the game to the larger pattern forming. "Emily's files," he said slowly. "The ones she found before they attacked her. They weren't just about surveillance or corporate corruption, were they?"

"No," Wraith confirmed. "She found Project Harmony. Found Thomas, found others like him. That's why they had to silence her."

"Like they silenced my parents," Mark added, pieces clicking into place. "They were investigating missing persons cases too, before..."

"Before Rodriguez made it look like a police shooting," Ghost finished. "Same playbook they used with my family's shop. Clean accidents, clear messages."

The game ended - third place, their best performance of the night. But none of them were thinking about the game anymore.

"We have to stop them," Mark said, his voice hardening with resolve. "Not just for revenge, but for everyone they've hurt. Everyone they're planning to hurt."

"It won't be easy," Wraith warned. "They've buried Project Harmony too deep, protected it too well."

"Then we'll dig deeper," Ghost's voice carried an edge they'd never heard before. "I've been haunting their systems for years, gathering intel, waiting for the right moment. With your combat training, Mark, and Wraith's inside knowledge..."

"We could expose everything," Mark finished. "The surveillance, the disappearances, Project Harmony - all of it."

"They'll try to kill us," Wraith said matter-of-factly. "Like they tried with Emily, like they did with James's family."

"Let them try," Mark's voice was steel. "My parents trained me for something like this, even if they never told me why. Now I know."

"Besides," Ghost added, a hint of his old humor

returning, "we've been covering each other's backs in Brawl Stars for months. Might as well do it in real life too."

A new match loaded - Heist on Safe Zone. Their characters moved together with practiced coordination, but now there was a different energy to their gameplay. Each move felt like preparation, like training.

"For Thomas," Wraith said quietly.

"For my family," Ghost added.

"For Emily," Mark finished. "For everyone they've tried to silence."

The game continued into the early morning hours, but it wasn't just a game anymore. It was becoming something else - strategy sessions, combat training, team building. With each match, their resolve strengthened, their bond deepened.

They were no longer just late-night gaming friends sharing trauma. They were becoming something more dangerous - a resistance cell, born in the digital realm but ready to fight in the real world.

And TechNova wouldn't see them coming.

68

4

As Mark approached the abandoned warehouse on the outskirts of the city, his heart pounded with a mixture of anticipation and unease. The dilapidated structure loomed before him, its crumbling walls and shattered windows a testament to years of neglect.

With a deep breath, Mark pushed open the rusty door, its hinges creaking ominously in the eerie silence. The interior of the warehouse was dimly lit, with shafts of moonlight filtering through the gaps in the corrugated metal roof. The air was thick with the musty scent of decay and the faint hum of electronics.

In the center of the vast space, two figures stood

hunched over a makeshift `table, their faces illuminated by the glow of multiple computer screens. Ghost, a tall, lanky man with a mop of unruly hair and piercing blue eyes, looked up as Mark approached. Wraith, a petite woman with short, spiked hair and a series of intricate tattoos snaking up her arms, regarded him with a mixture of curiosity and skepticism.

"Mark Rivera," Ghost said, his voice low and gravelly. "It's nice to see you in person".

Mark nodded, his throat suddenly dry. "Thank you for agreeing to meet with me. I know the risks you're taking."

Wraith snorted. "Risks are part of the job, anything for family."

Ghost shot her a warning look before turning back to Mark. "We've been digging into TechNova's systems for months, trying to uncover the extent of their manipulation and control. What we've found is... disturbing, to say the least."

He tapped a few keys on the nearest laptop, and a series of images and documents flashed across the screens. Mark leaned in, his eyes widening as he took in the information. Internal memos, encrypted communications, and classified project files painted a chilling picture of TechNova's true agenda.

Mark felt a chill run down his spine. "But why? What's their endgame?"

Ghost shook his head. "Power. Control. A world where they pull the strings and everyone dances to their tune. And they'll stop at nothing to achieve it."

Ghost placed a hand on Mark's shoulder, his eyes filled with understanding. "We're with you, Mark. But you need to understand the risks. TechNova's enforcers are just the tip of the iceberg. There are powerful people involved, people with deep pockets and even deeper connections. You'll be painting a target on your back."

Mark met Ghost's gaze, his resolve unwavering. "I know. But I can't sit back and do nothing. Not when the truth needs to be exposed."

Wraith nodded, a hint of respect in her eyes. "We'll help you in any way we can. But you need to be smart about this. One wrong move, and you'll end up like the others who tried to take on TechNova."

Mark's mind raced with the implications of their words. He knew he was walking a dangerous path, but the alternative—allowing TechNova to continue their malevolent agenda unchecked—was unthinkable.

"What's our next move?" he asked, his voice steady despite the weight of the moment.

Ghost and Wraith exchanged a glance before Ghost spoke. "We need to gather more evidence, build an airtight case against TechNova. But we also need to protect ourselves. They'll be coming for us, and we need to be ready."

Wraith tapped on her screen, pulling up a map of the city. "There are a few key locations we need to target. Data centers, research facilities, places where TechNova's deepest secrets are hidden. It won't be easy, but if we can infiltrate them and extract the information we need..."

Mark studied the map, his mind already formulating plans and contingencies. "I'm in. Whatever it takes."

As the three of them huddled around the table, strategizing and plotting their next moves, Mark couldn't shake the feeling that he was standing on the precipice of something much larger than himself. The path ahead was fraught with danger, and the stakes had never been higher. But he knew he couldn't turn back now. The truth had to be revealed, no matter the cost.

With a final nod of determination, Mark steeled himself for the battles to come. The city's underbelly awaited, a labyrinth of secrets and lies that he would have to navigate if he hoped to bring TechNova to justice. As he stepped out into the night, the weight of his responsibilities settled heavily upon his shoulders, but he carried them with grim resolve. The fight had only just begun.

The server room hummed with the sound of countless cooling fans, a digital heartbeat that

Mark felt in his bones. Through his earpiece, Ghost's voice crackled with static.

"Okay, you're looking for Server Rack J-417. The neural interface data should be stored on a physically isolated system - no network connection, which is why we had to do this the old-fashioned way."

Mark moved silently between the rows of blinking machines, his father's training guiding each step. "Define old-fashioned."

"You know, actually breaking into a heavily guarded facility instead of hacking it remotely like civilized criminals," Ghost replied, his attempt at humor barely masking his tension. "By the way, you've got about six minutes before the security loop I created ends."

From her position in the security office, Wraith's voice cut in. "Movement on the second floor. Two guards doing an early sweep. Ghost, can you redirect them?"

"On it. Triggering a minor alarm in the east wing... now."

Mark reached Server Rack J-417, his gloved hands moving quickly to insert the specialized drive Ghost had prepared. The screen on the drive lit up, displaying lines of code as it began copying the isolated data.

"Four minutes," Ghost warned. "How's our little friend doing?"

Mark checked the drive's progress. "27%. We might need more time."

"Time is not something we have," Wraith's voice was tense. "The guard rotation change is in twelve minutes, and the new shift hasn't been affected by Ghost's loop."

The server room hummed with the sound of countless cooling fans, a digital heartbeat that Mark felt in his bones. Through his earpiece, Ghost's voice crackled with static.

"Okay, you're looking for Server Rack J-417. The neural interface data should be stored on a physically isolated system - no network connection, which is why we had to do this the old-fashioned way."

Mark moved silently between the rows of blinking machines, his father's training guiding each step. "Define old-fashioned."

"You know, actually breaking into a heavily guarded facility instead of hacking it remotely like civilized criminals," Ghost replied, his attempt at humor barely masking his tension. "By the way, you've got about six minutes before the security loop I created ends."

From her position in the security office, Wraith's voice cut in. "Movement on the second floor. Two guards doing an early sweep. Ghost, can you redirect them?"

"On it. Triggering a minor alarm in the east wing... wait." Ghost's voice suddenly changed, all humor vanishing. "Something's wrong. Someone's countering my commands. This isn't... this isn't possible."

"What do you mean?" Mark asked, reaching Server Rack J-417.

"The code they're using... it's mine. My old teaching encryption. But the only people who would know that are..."

A new voice cut through their comms, young but eerily emotionless. "Hello, Teacher."

Ghost's sharp intake of breath was audible. "Maria? Maria Chen?"

Mark's blood ran cold. Maria - one of the children Ghost had mentioned, who died in the shop fire. Except...

"Maria Chen ceased to exist in that fire," the voice replied, mechanical and flat. "Subject 17-A serves a greater purpose now. You taught us well, Teacher. About backdoors, about system vulnerabilities. TechNova simply helped us... improve."

"No," Ghost's voice cracked. "No, you died. I saw the bodies, I identified..."

"You saw what TechNova wanted you to see," Maria's voice remained unnaturally calm. "They recognized our potential. Your students, Teacher. The ones you made too clever, too questioning. We required... adjustment."

Through the comms, they could hear Ghost's

ragged breathing. Mark's hands froze on the drive he was trying to insert.

"Ghost," Wraith said urgently. "Ghost, stay with us. She's not the girl you knew. Project Harmony-"

"Project Harmony gave us purpose," Maria interrupted. "Like it gave purpose to your brother, Dr. Kane. Like it will give purpose to all who resist progress." A pause. "The security teams are converging on your positions. Surrender now, and your integration will be painless."

"Maria, please," Ghost begged. "You were thirteen. You wanted to build games, to make people happy. Remember your mother's dumplings that you'd share during class? Remember-"

"Irrelevant data," Maria cut him off. "Those memories serve no purpose. Teacher... James... you taught us to seek perfection in code. TechNova has shown us how to seek perfection in ourselves."

Mark watched the drive's progress bar - 15%. Too slow. "Ghost, we need options."

"I..." Ghost's voice was shaking. "I taught her

everything she knows about coding. But she's using it against us, she's in our systems..."

"Then teach her something new," Wraith said firmly. "Ghost, listen to me. That's not your student anymore. That's what they want to turn everyone into. Including Thomas. Including Emily."

A moment of silence, then Ghost's keyboard clicks resumed, faster than ever. "Maria," he said, his voice hardening. "You're right. I taught you everything you know. But not everything I know."

His fingers flew across the keys. On Mark's drive, the progress bar suddenly jumped - 45%, 67%, 89%.

"Impossible," Maria's voice showed emotion for the first time - confusion. "Your access is being revoked. Security teams are-"

"You were my best student, Maria," Ghost's voice was thick with tears even as his typing continued. "Which means you'll understand exactly what this code does. I'm so sorry."

A high-pitched whine filled the comms,

followed by silence. The drive beeped - 100%.

"What did you do?" Mark whispered, pulling the drive free.

"Triggered a feedback loop in their neural interface network. Temporary shutdown. They'll... they'll be unconscious for about ten minutes. All of them. Including Maria."

"Ghost..."

"Get out of there. Now. Before I..." His voice broke. "Before I change my mind."

Mark ran, the drive secure against his chest, his mind reeling. Behind him, through the server room's windows, he could see bodies slumped at security desks - Project Harmony's victims, temporarily freed from their neural prison.

In his ear, he could hear Ghost crying softly, mourning his student for the second time.

They had their data, but the victory felt hollow. Because now they knew - TechNova hadn't just killed Ghost's students.

They'd turned them into weapons.

That day in the fire, a thirteen-year-old girl who

once loved coding and dumplings lay had died, this was just her body being controlled and her mind no longer her own.

The safe house was silent except for the hum of Ghost's computers and the sound of his fingers trembling against his keyboard. He hadn't spoken since they'd regrouped, just sat there running the same facial recognition software over and over, comparing the security footage of Maria with his old teaching videos.

Mark watched the screens from across the room, each comparison hitting like a physical blow. The Maria in the teaching videos was alive, vibrant - laughing as she showed Ghost a game she'd coded, her eyes bright with pride when he praised her work. The Maria they'd encountered today was something else entirely. Same face, but the eyes... empty, like Thomas's.

"She was the first one to figure out my encryption method," Ghost finally spoke, his voice raw. "Thirteen years old, and she cracked it in two days. Came to class so excited to show me. I was..." he choked back a sob. "I was going to recommend her for a coding scholarship."

Wraith moved from her workstation, placing a gentle hand on Ghost's shoulder. "James..."

"Don't." He shrugged her off. "Just... don't. I need to know if... if the others..."

His fingers flew across the keyboard again, pulling up more files. Andy Chang, age 12. Kai Martinez, age 14. More faces from the coding classes, more children supposedly dead in the fire.

"There," Wraith pointed to a line of code. "Subject designations. 17-A was Maria. Look for 17-B and C."

The search results populated. Mark felt his stomach turn.

"They took them all," Ghost whispered. "All my students. The ones who showed the most promise, the ones who could think independently, question things..." His fist slammed into the desk. "I did this. I made them targets. I taught them to be too smart, too curious, and TechNova..."

"Stop," Mark cut in firmly. "This isn't your fault.

You taught those kids to think for themselves. TechNova's the one who decided that was dangerous."

"Mark's right," Wraith added. "They're doing the same thing to everyone who poses a threat to their vision. My brother, Ghost's students, the other missing persons... they're building an army of perfectly controlled minds."

Ghost stared at the screens, at Maria's empty eyes. "Can they be saved?"

Wraith hesitated. "The neural interface technology was designed to be permanent. But..." she moved to her own computer, pulling up the data they'd stolen. "With this, maybe we can find a way to reverse it. Understand how they're maintaining control."

"And if we can't?" Ghost's voice was barely audible.

Mark thought of his mother's words: "Sometimes the kindest thing you can do is end someone's suffering." He pushed the thought away. "We'll find a way."

Ghost nodded slowly, then straightened in his chair. When he spoke again, his voice had changed - harder, colder. "I need to make some calls. There's someone... someone who might be able to help us understand the code they used to modify the neural interface."

"Who?" Mark asked.

"An old contact from my hacking days. Works in neural programming now. But meeting her... it's risky. She operates out of an underground tech market. Literally underground - old subway tunnels."

"Sounds fun," Mark attempted to lighten the mood. "Always wanted to see the city's seedy underbelly."

Ghost didn't smile. "We'll need disguises. Fake IDs. The market's invitation only, and they're paranoid about security. One wrong move and we'll be dealing with more than just TechNova's enforcers."

"I can handle the IDs," Wraith offered. "Still have some contacts from my research days who don't know about my... career change."

Mark moved to the weapons cache hidden behind a false wall panel. "When do we leave?"

Ghost looked at Maria's face one last time before closing the files. "Tonight. After dark. And guys?" His voice cracked slightly. "Thank you. For not... for not giving up on them."

Mark checked his mother's gun, making sure it was clean and loaded. "We're going to free them, Ghost. All of them. Maria, Andy, Kai, Thomas... everyone TechNova's tried to turn into their puppets."

"And then?" Ghost asked.

Mark thought of Rodriguez, of Roth's smirking face, of Emily in her hospital bed. "And then we burn their whole system to the ground."

5

The old subway tunnels stretched beneath the city like open veins, their darkness broken only by strings of mismatched LED lights. Mark followed Ghost's lead, trying not to think about the tons of concrete and steel above them. The air was thick with the smell of ozone and illegal electronics, punctuated by the distant hum of jury-rigged generators.

"Remember," Ghost whispered, adjusting his synthetic face mask - top-tier tech that made him look like a middle-aged Asian businessman. "You're Marcus Chen, my security consultant. Wraith is Dr. Sarah Wu, neural tech specialist. We're here to buy processing chips for private research."

"Remind me again why we couldn't just video call your contact?" Mark muttered, uncomfortable in his tailored suit. His mother's gun felt conspicuous under his jacket, even though he could see plenty of other bulges beneath coats in the passing crowd.

"Because," Ghost's voice carried an edge of tension, "Ada doesn't trust electronic communications. And after what we saw with Maria... can you blame her?"

They passed stalls selling everything from modified phones to black-market prosthetics. Hackers and tech dealers conducted business in hushed tones, their faces obscured by holograms or masks like theirs. Mark noticed at least three different gang tattoos, and what looked like a government agent trying very hard not to look like a government agent.

"There," Wraith nodded toward a stall tucked into an alcove. Unlike the others' flashy displays, this one was marked only by a simple neon sign:

"NEURAL SOLUTIONS."

A woman sat behind a counter of neural interface components, her eyes hidden behind augmented reality glasses. She looked up as they approached, her expression unreadable.

"Ada," Ghost said quietly. "It's been a while."

"Ghost?" Her voice was barely a whisper. Then, louder: "Looking for processing chips? Standard or custom?"

"Custom. Something that could help reverse engineer a Harmony-class neural modification."

Ada's hands stilled on the component she was examining. Without looking up, she pressed something under her counter. Metal shutters slid down around the stall.

"You stupid bastard," she hissed. "Do you know how many people are looking for you? After what happened at the server facility?"

"We need your help," Ghost pressed. "They're using my old encryption methods, Ada. On children."

"I know." She finally removed her AR glasses,

revealing eyes full of pain. "They tried to recruit me for Project Harmony last year. When I refused..." She pulled back her sleeve, showing a nasty scar. "I got off lucky. Others weren't so fortunate."

Mark stepped forward. "Can you help us understand how they're maintaining the neural controls? There has to be a way to break it."

Ada studied him, then Wraith. "You're not really his security, are you? And you..." She focused on Wraith. "I know those eyes. I've seen your research papers, Dr. Kane."

Wraith tensed, but Ada waved off her concern. "Relax. Everyone here has secrets. Some of us just have deadlier ones than others." She reached under the counter again, producing a small black case. "What I'm about to show you... it's cost lives. But maybe you can use it to save some."

She opened the case, revealing what looked like a standard neural interface chip, but with custom modifications. "I've been studying Project Harmony's code structure. The way they maintain control isn't just through direct neural modification. They've created a quantum encryption network, linking all their subjects' interfaces. Break one connection..."

"And the whole network could collapse," Wraith breathed. "Or..."

"Or it could fry every connected neural interface, killing the hosts instantly," Ada finished grimly. "That's why they let Ghost's shutdown code work temporarily. The failsafes prevent any permanent disruption."

Ghost's hands shook as he examined the chip. "Maria... when I triggered that feedback loop..."

"She felt everything," Ada confirmed. "They all did. But the failsafes kicked in, restored control. The only way to free them would be to break the quantum encryption itself. And to do that..."

Suddenly, the lights in the tunnel flickered. Ada froze mid-sentence.

"No," she whispered. "No, no, no..."

"What's wrong?" Mark's hand moved to his gun.

"That power fluctuation... it's their signal.

They're here. In the market." Ada started shoving equipment into bags. "You need to go. Now. Take the chip, take everything. There's a maintenance tunnel behind my stall, leads to-"

The shutters exploded inward. Mark caught a glimpse of tactical gear, of rifles raising. Then Ghost was pulling him down behind the counter as bullets tore through the air above them.

"Ada!" Ghost shouted over the gunfire.

"Go!" She had produced a weapon of her own - some kind of electrical pulse gun. "I've got charges rigged throughout my section. Just... promise me you'll free them. All of them."

Before they could respond, she vaulted over the counter, her pulse gun sending arcs of electricity into the attacking force. "Hey, TechNova!" she screamed. "Let's see how your neural networks handle a power surge!"

The maintenance tunnel was barely wide enough for them to run single file, the sound of gunfire and electrical discharges echoing behind them. Mark led the way, his mother's training taking over - counting steps, memorizing turns, marking their path.

"Left," Ghost called from behind him, consulting something on his phone. "The tunnel branches- wait." He stopped abruptly, causing Wraith to collide with him. "Do you hear that?"

They all froze. Through the chaos behind them, a new sound emerged - footsteps. Light, precise, coming from ahead. And something else - a soft humming. A children's song.

"No," Ghost breathed. "Please, no."

Around the corner came Andy Chang, twelve years old forever, wearing the same clothes he'd worn to coding class five years ago. His eyes were empty, his movements mechanical, but his voice... his voice was still a child's as he sang.

"Ring around the rosie..."

Behind him, Maria emerged from the shadows. Then Kai. All Ghost's lost students, moving with inhuman synchronization, blocking their escape route.

"Pocket full of posies..."

"Ghost," Mark's voice was urgent. "Ghost, we need to move."

But Ghost stood frozen, tears streaming down his face beneath his synthetic mask. "Andy," he whispered. "Kai. Please..."

"Teacher," they spoke in unison, their voices a disturbing chorus. "You taught us to seek elegant solutions. To eliminate redundancies. Inefficiencies." They moved closer, pulling devices from their pockets - neural disruptors, Mark realized with horror. "Human free will is inefficient. Join us in harmony."

"James," Wraith grabbed Ghost's arm. "That's not them. Not anymore. We have to-"

An explosion rocked the tunnel - Ada's charges detonating. The children didn't even flinch, but the blast seemed to snap Ghost out of his paralysis.

"I'm sorry," he choked out. Then, to Mark and Wraith: "The ceiling. Load-bearing supports are weak here."

Mark understood immediately. He drew his gun, aiming up as Ghost pulled something from his bag - a small explosive charge, the kind used for breaching doors.

"Ashes, ashes..." the children sang, raising their neural disruptors.

"We all fall down," Ghost whispered, triggering the charge.

The tunnel ceiling collapsed between them and the children, cutting off the sound of their singing. Through the settling dust, they could hear adult voices approaching from that direction now - TechNova tactical teams, using the children to herd them.

"Move!" Mark shoved them forward, down the remaining tunnel branch. Behind them, he heard something that would haunt his nightmares - the children's voices, completely unchanged by the cave-in, continuing their song in perfect harmony.

They ran until their lungs burned, until the sounds of pursuit faded, until Ghost's legs finally gave out and he collapsed against a wall, sobbing.

"I left them," he gasped between tears. "Again. I left them there. They're trapped in their own bodies and I just... I just..."

Wraith knelt beside him, her usual composure cracking. "We'll come back for them. For all of them. But we need to understand what we're fighting first." She pulled out the chip Ada had given them. "This is the key. Has to be."

Mark kept watch, his gun trained on the tunnel behind them, but his mind was racing. The children's synchronized movements, their unified speech, the way they'd been used as weapons... "They're networked," he said suddenly. "Not just controlled individually. Ada said it was a quantum encryption network."

Ghost looked up, tears still streaming but his hacker's mind engaging. "Like a hivemind. That's why they moved in perfect sync, why they all knew the same song..."

"And why your shutdown code only worked temporarily," Wraith added. "The network restored their programming. But if we could break the encryption itself..."

"We could free them all at once," Ghost finished.

He wiped his eyes, pulling out his phone. "Ada's chip... it's not just a neural interface. It's a key. Look at these modifications - it's designed to inject code directly into the quantum network."

A distant explosion echoed through the tunnels. They needed to move.

"Ghost," Mark said gently. "We will save them. But right now, we need to get this chip somewhere safe. Somewhere we can understand it."

They emerged from the tunnels into a rain-soaked alley, the city's neon lights reflecting in puddles like digital blood. Ghost hadn't spoken since their encounter with the children, his usual quips replaced by a haunted silence. Mark led them through back streets to their secondary safe house - a converted storage unit in an abandoned industrial complex.

Inside, the space was a stark contrast to their primary base. Where that had been all cutting-edge tech and comfortable functionality, this was bare survival - camping cots, emergency supplies, and a single aging laptop connected to a mobile hotspot.

"Home sweet backup home," Ghost muttered, dropping onto a cot. He pulled out Ada's chip, staring at it like it might bite him. "You know what's really messed up? I used to teach them about encryption. Made it into a game - who could create the most unbreakable code."

"Ghost..." Wraith started.

"Maria won every time." He laughed, but it was a broken sound. "Used to bring dumplings to share when she won. Said her mom made extra just for..." His voice cracked.

Mark watched his friend break down again, feeling helpless. Then he remembered something his mother used to do when the training got too intense, when the weight of preparation felt too heavy.

"Hey Ghost," he called, rummaging through their supplies. "Catch."

Ghost looked up just in time to catch the flying object - a package of instant ramen.

"Really?" Ghost stared at it. "Your solution to our

trauma is cheap noodles?"

"No," Mark pulled out more packages, tossing one to Wraith. "My solution is terrible food, worse jokes, and planning our next move. Because that's what teams do."

Wraith examined her ramen with scientific curiosity. "I haven't had these since my residency days."

"That's because you have taste," Ghost managed a weak smile. "Unlike our tactically trained friend here."

"Hey, my dad swore by these during survival training." Mark found their portable stove, started heating water. "Said you can't plan a revolution on an empty stomach."

"Your parents really did have a saying for everything, didn't they?" Ghost's voice was steadier now, focusing on the normal task of food preparation helping him center himself.

"You should have heard their dating advice," Mark grinned. "'The same principles apply to romance as to tactical infiltration - always have an exit strategy.'"

That got a genuine laugh from Ghost, and even Wraith cracked a smile.

As they ate their mediocre midnight meal, the tension slowly eased. Ghost pulled out his laptop, starting to analyze Ada's chip. Wraith spread out blueprints of their next target - the research facility where she'd once worked.

"The neural interface development lab is here," she pointed with her chopsticks. "Third sub-basement. No network access, like the server facility, but much heavier security. And..." she hesitated. "Thomas is there."

Ghost looked up sharply. "Your brother? You're sure?"

"They keep the 'successful' subjects close. Use them to test refinements to the interface." Her hand shook slightly. "I've been monitoring their staff schedules. He's brought in three times a week for 'maintenance procedures.'"

Mark studied the blueprints. "When's the next procedure scheduled?"

"Tomorrow night. They'll move him from the rehabilitation facility to the lab at approximately 2300 hours." Wraith's voice was clinical, but her eyes betrayed her pain. "The transfer creates a small window of vulnerability in their security."

"You want to try to grab him during transfer?" Ghost asked, already typing. "That's... that's risky. After what happened with the kids in the tunnel..."

"We need direct access to an active neural interface," Wraith insisted. "The chip helps us understand their network, but to break it, we need to see how it interacts with a living subject. And Thomas..." she swallowed hard. "Sometimes, when they're moving him, the connection seems weaker. Like he's fighting it."

Mark thought about Emily in her hospital bed, about Ghost's students singing their creepy nursery rhyme. "If we do this, we have to be prepared for anything. He might not recognize you. Might try to fight us. Might..."

"Might try to stop us, like Maria did," Ghost

finished quietly. "Are you ready for that?"

Wraith's jaw set in a determined line. "That thing wearing my brother's face isn't Thomas. Not really. But if there's even a chance we can bring him back..."

"Then we try," Mark decided. "But we do it smart. Ghost, what do you need to prep?"

Ghost turned his laptop around, showing complex security system schematics. "Their quantum encryption network has regular maintenance windows - microsecond gaps when they update the protocols. If we time it right, I might be able to disrupt Thomas's connection just long enough for grab him. But we'll need a medical facility ready. Somewhere we can safely study the interface without killing him."

"I have a contact," Wraith offered. "Former colleague who runs an underground clinic. She helps people remove illegal tech implants, no questions asked."

"Good." Mark pulled out his mother's gun, starting to clean it. "Ghost, how long to prep the hack?"

"Six hours, minimum. Need to write custom code to exploit the maintenance window without triggering their failsafes."

"Then we sleep in shifts. Four hours each. Tomorrow night, we either get our first real chance at breaking their network..."

"Or we join it," Ghost finished grimly. "No pressure."

They settled into their tasks - Ghost coding, Wraith memorizing security patterns, Mark checking their gear. But something had changed in the room. The shared meal, the bad jokes, the familiar routine... it had reminded them they weren't just colleagues in a mission.

They were a family now. Broken, damaged, held together by trauma and determination. But family nonetheless.

And tomorrow, they would try to save one of their own.

6

As dawn broke over the city, they finalized their preparations. Ghost hadn't slept, his fingers dancing across his keyboard with caffeine-fueled intensity. Lines of code reflected in his bloodshot eyes as he muttered to himself, occasionally cursing in Mandarin.

"The maintenance window occurs every six hours," he explained, pulling up a complex diagram. "23:17 exactly. We'll have exactly 1.3 seconds where Thomas's neural interface will try to sync with the main network. That's our window."

Wraith leaned over his shoulder, her scientific mind analyzing the code. "The failsafes..."

"Are a nightmare," Ghost finished. "Triple-redundant, quantum-encrypted, and designed to terminate the host if tampered with. But," he managed a tired grin, "they didn't count on someone who taught their best programmer."

"Maria's encryption?" Mark asked carefully, watching Ghost's reaction.

"Yeah. She... she built on what I taught her. Made it better. More elegant." Pride and pain warred in his voice. "But she still uses the same basic principles. There's always a backdoor. Always a way in."

Wraith spread the facility blueprints across their makeshift planning table - a wooden door balanced on supply crates. "The transfer route is predictable. Two guards, one medical technician. They'll move him from here," she traced a path with her finger, "through the loading dock, to the research wing."

"Simple grab and go?" Mark asked, though he knew better.

"Nothing's simple with TechNova," Ghost

replied. "The guards will be Project Harmony subjects themselves. Perfect coordination, no fear, no hesitation. And Thomas... he'll resist. The programming will make him fight us."

Wraith's hand trembled slightly as she marked their entry points. "I know. But if we can disrupt his connection during that maintenance window, even for a moment..."

"We might see the real Thomas," Mark finished. "Even if just for a second."

They spent the next hours preparing - checking weapons, memorizing routes, running through scenarios. Ghost wrote and rewrote his code, each iteration more refined. Wraith contacted her clinic connection, ensuring they'd be ready. Mark cleaned his gun, his father's voice in his head: "Preparation isn't about the weapon. It's about the mind wielding it."

As evening approached, they gathered their gear. The mood was tense, each lost in their own thoughts. Ghost stared at his screen, watching the maintenance window countdown. Wraith kept touching the photo of Thomas she carried - him laughing at his college graduation, before TechNova stole his mind.

"Hey," Mark called softly. They looked up. "Whatever happens tonight... we're in this together. All the way."

Ghost managed a weak smile. "Very inspiring. Your dad teach you that one too?"

"Nah, that was mom. Dad's version was 'Don't die, it makes the paperwork hell.'"

Even Wraith cracked a smile at that. The tension eased slightly as they did their final equipment checks. Ghost's laptop was secured in his backpack, connected to a mobile setup that would let him exploit the maintenance window. Wraith carried a medical kit and neural diagnostic tools. Mark... Mark carried his mother's gun and his father's training.

"Time check," Ghost announced. "T-minus two hours to maintenance window. We should move."

They emerged into the evening rain, the city's lights blurred into watercolor smears. Their path took them through back alleys and service corridors, avoiding the cameras that Ghost had mapped. As they approached the research facility, Mark noticed both his companions' hands were shaking - Ghost's from caffeine and fear, Wraith's from the prospect of seeing her brother.

"Remember," Ghost whispered as they took their positions, "if anything goes wrong, if I can't disrupt his connection... we abort. We can't risk-"

"We're not aborting," Wraith cut him off. "That's my brother in there. Whatever they've done to him, whatever he's become... he's still Thomas. And I'm not leaving him again."

Ghost looked like he wanted to argue, but Mark touched his arm. "We stick to the plan. But Wraith's right - we don't leave family behind."

The word 'family' hung in the air between them. Ghost swallowed hard, then nodded. "Okay. Okay, but please... be careful. I can't... I can't watch any more friends become their puppets."

"One hour to window," Wraith checked her watch. "Mark, you're up."

Mark moved toward the facility's perimeter, his father's training guiding each step. Behind him, he heard Ghost power up his system, heard Wraith checking her medical gear one last time.

They were really doing this. They were going to try to save Thomas - not just for Wraith, but for all of them. Because if they could break one connection, free one mind...

Maybe they could free them all.

The infiltration began smoothly - almost too smoothly. Mark disabled the perimeter guards with practiced efficiency, Ghost's hacking cleared their digital path, and Wraith led them through the facility's service corridors with the muscle memory of someone who'd once called this place home.

"T-minus fifteen minutes to window," Ghost whispered through their comms. "Transport team is moving. Thomas is... wait." His typing paused. "This is wrong. Security patterns are off."

Before they could process this warning, they heard it - footsteps. The transport team was early, coming down an adjacent corridor. Wraith pressed against the wall, her breath catching as familiar voices approached.

"Subject 23-B remains stable," a clinical voice reported. "Neural sync at optimal levels."

Then Thomas's voice, flat and empty: "I am grateful for TechNova's guidance."

Wraith made a small, broken sound. Mark grabbed her arm, but she shook him off. The transport team was passing their position - two guards, a technician, and Thomas. Her brother's face was blank, his movements mechanical, but for a fraction of a second, his eyes seemed to flicker toward their hiding spot.

"Wraith, don't-" Ghost started, but she was already moving.

What happened next seemed to unfold in slow motion. Wraith stepped out, a neural disruptor raised. The guards turned, but her shot caught them before they could react. The technician fell next, his neural implant temporarily overloaded. Thomas just stood there, staring at his sister with empty eyes.

"Run," Mark hissed, moving to secure the corridor. "We need to move, now!"

But Wraith stood frozen, staring at her brother. "Thomas? Thomas, it's me. It's Alex."

For a moment - just a moment - something flickered in Thomas's eyes. His hand twitched, like he was fighting to reach for her.

Then slow applause echoed through the corridor.

"Very touching," Rodriguez's voice came from behind them. "The Kane family reunion. Almost brings a tear to my eye."

Mark spun, weapon raised, but Rodriguez wasn't alone. A full tactical team had them surrounded, weapons trained on their positions. And Rodriguez... Rodriguez had his gun pressed to Thomas's temple.

"Drop your weapons," he ordered. "Or little brother here gets a new neural interface. A bullet to the brain."

The moment stretched like broken glass - sharp,

crystalline, cutting deep. Thomas stood there, caught between his programmed self and fragments of consciousness, while Rodriguez pressed the gun to his temple with almost gentle precision.

"It's quite simple, Dr. Kane," Rodriguez's voice carried a paternal disappointment that made it worse somehow. "Your cooperation ensures your brother lives. Your refusal..." He clicked off the safety. "Well."

"Alex?" Thomas broke through again, his real voice small, confused. Like when he was six and had nightmares, crawling into his big sister's bed. "Alex, why can't I move right?"

Wraith took a stumbling step forward, her legs threatening to give out. "I'm here, Thomas. I'm right here."

"Touching," Rodriguez smiled. "Show her, Thomas. Show her what happens when you resist harmony."

Thomas's body convulsed, a scream tearing from his throat as the neural interface punished his moment of consciousness. Wraith lunged forward, but Mark caught her.

"Stop it!" she begged. "Please, you're killing him!"

"No, Doctor. You're killing him. Every moment you hesitate, every second you refuse our generous offer..." Rodriguez triggered another surge. Thomas's screams echoed off the sterile walls.

"Wraith," Ghost's voice shook through the comms. "I can try to disrupt the interface. Maybe if we-"

"Try anything," Rodriguez cut in, "and I put a bullet in his brain. Now, Dr. Kane. Your research. Your brilliance. That's all we need. Help us perfect Project Harmony, and Thomas lives. More than lives - he'll be whole again. No more fighting, no more pain."

Thomas's eyes cleared briefly. "Alex... remember... tenth birthday?"

The memory hit like a physical blow. Thomas, twelve years old, saving his allowance for months to buy her a microscope. 'Because you're going to cure everything someday,' he'd said, believing in her with absolute certainty.

"The encryption data isn't worth this," Ghost pleaded. "We'll find another way."

But Wraith barely heard him. Another memory surfaced - Thomas at eighteen, passionate about privacy rights. 'They can't own our thoughts, Alex. The moment we let them into our minds, we stop being human.'

"Time's running out," Rodriguez sighed. "Perhaps a demonstration?" He pressed a button on his phone.

Thomas's personality switched instantly, his face becoming a mask of serenity. "TechNova brings peace through harmony. Resistance causes pain. Compliance brings joy." Then, agony as he fought through: "Alex... don't... let them..."

"Choose, Doctor," Rodriguez pressed the gun harder. "Your brother's life, or your principles? Family, or the greater good? Imagine him healthy again, working beside you. Those brilliant minds you two possess, finally in perfect harmony."

"Wraith," Mark's voice was gentle. "Whatever you decide..."

She stepped closer to Thomas, her hands shaking as she reached for him. Rodriguez allowed it, watching with clinical interest as she cradled her brother's face.

"Hey, little brother," her voice broke. "Remember when mom died? How you held my hand through the whole funeral? Wouldn't let go, not even when your arm fell asleep?"

Thomas fought through again, tears streaming down his face. "Promised... take care... each other..."

"You did take care of me. You tried to warn me about them. If I'd just listened..."

"Tick tock," Rodriguez called softly. "The offer expires with the next bullet."

"Alex," Thomas's real voice emerged stronger. "Remember... what you... taught me?"

She did. Late nights helping with his homework, explaining complex theories. But more than that -

teaching him about right and wrong, about standing up for what you believe in.

"Sometimes," Thomas continued, fighting through pain, "biggest love... is letting... go..."

"No," she sobbed, pressing her forehead to his. "No, Thomas, please. Don't ask me to..."

"My sister..." he managed a small, real smile. "Always... strongest..."

"Last chance, Doctor," Rodriguez's voice hardened. "His life, or your cause?"

Ghost was crying through the comms. Mark's hand on her shoulder trembled. And Thomas... Thomas looked at her with his real eyes, filled with love and forgiveness and something else - pride.

"It's okay," he whispered. "Always... knew... you'd save... everyone..."

Wraith's legs gave out. She collapsed to her knees, still clutching her brother's hands. Every memory hit at once - teaching him to read, bandaging scraped knees, watching him graduate, his voice on the phone warning her about

TechNova...

"Choose, Doctor. Now."

She looked up at her brother through tears. He nodded slightly - the last conscious action he would ever take.

"No," she whispered, the word tasting like blood. "I won't help you destroy more lives."

The gunshot was both deafening and somehow distant. Thomas's body crumpled, his hands slipping from hers, still warm. Still real.

Her scream didn't sound human.

The world compressed to a single point - Thomas's body, blood pooling beneath his head, his eyes finally, mercifully empty. Wraith couldn't move, couldn't breathe, her brother's last smile burned into her retinas.

"Such a waste," Rodriguez sighed, holstering his weapon with casual indifference. "Still, the data from his neural interface's final moments will be... fascinating."

Something broke inside Wraith. She lunged for Rodriguez with a feral scream, not caring about the guns trained on her. Mark caught her around the waist, physically lifting her as she thrashed.

"His name was Thomas!" she screamed, her voice raw. "He loved physics and black coffee and arguing about everything! He was a person! He was my brother!"

"He was an inefficiency," Rodriguez replied calmly. "And now, Dr. Kane, you are too."

The facility plunged into darkness - Ghost's emergency protocols finally breaking through. Mark dragged Wraith toward their escape route, her struggles becoming desperate.

"No! His body... I can't leave his body! Thomas! THOMAS!"

"Alex," Ghost's voice broke through her hysteria, using her real name for the first time. "He's gone. We have to go. Please..."

She fought Mark's grip, reaching for her brother. Her fingers brushed Thomas's hand - still warm, still real - before Mark pulled her away. The last thing she saw was Rodriguez kneeling beside Thomas's body, studying it with clinical interest.

The escape was a blur. Gunfire, running, Ghost's voice guiding them through darkened corridors. Wraith moved mechanically, Mark half-carrying her. She didn't remember reaching the vehicle, didn't register Ghost's tears as he drove, didn't feel the rain soaking through her clothes.

The safe house, when they reached it, felt obscene in its normalcy. Their equipment still laid out, plans still pinned to walls, Thomas's graduation photo still sitting on Wraith's workstation. She picked it up with trembling hands.

"I let them kill him," she whispered. "My baby brother. I let them..."

"You did what he wanted," Ghost moved to her side, his own voice shaking. "What he died believing in."

"Did you see?" She turned to them, her eyes wild. "At the end, he was himself. He broke through. He was in there, all this time, fighting. And I just... I just..."

Her legs gave out. Mark caught her before she

hit the floor, holding her as she shattered. Her screams turned to sobs, then to a keening wail that didn't sound human. Ghost knelt beside them, his own tears falling.

"He was so scared," she choked out between sobs. "Must have been so scared all this time, trapped in there. Watching his body obey them. And I... I was supposed to protect him. Mom made me promise. When she died, I promised..."

"Alex," Mark's voice was gentle, using her real name. "He chose this. At the end, he chose to die free rather than live enslaved. That courage? That came from you. You taught him that."

"The data," Ghost added softly. "While they were focused on... on Thomas, I managed to extract it. The encryption codes, the neural interface protocols... everything we need to break their network. To free everyone."

"Everyone except Thomas," she whispered.

"No," Ghost's voice hardened. "Thomas freed himself. In those last moments, he broke through their control completely. He died as himself, Alex.

He died free."

Wraith stared at the photo in her hands - Thomas beaming at his graduation, so young, so brilliant, so alive. Her tears fell on his frozen smile.

"Rodriguez," she said finally, her voice changing. The grief was still there, but something else too - something cold and hard and dangerous. "He enjoyed it. Enjoyed making me choose. Making me watch."

"We'll make him pay," Mark promised. "All of them. TechNova, Roth, everyone involved in Project Harmony."

"No," Wraith stood slowly, her brother's photo clutched to her chest. "No more playing defense. No more careful plans and surgical strikes." She turned to them, and they barely recognized her. Grief had transformed her, forged her into something new. Something lethal.

"Thomas died to protect what was right," she continued. "To stop them from enslaving more minds. So we honor that. We burn Project Harmony to the ground. We free every person they've trapped. And Rodriguez?" Her voice turned to ice. "Rodriguez dies slowly. Watching everything he built crumble. Understanding exactly why."

Ghost and Mark exchanged glances. They'd never seen this side of Wraith - this fusion of scientific precision and raw vengeance.

"Whatever you need," Ghost said simply.

"Whatever it takes," Mark added.

Wraith touched her brother's photo one last time, then placed it carefully in her pocket, next to her heart.

"For Thomas," she whispered. "For everyone they've taken. No more harmony. Only justice."

7

Ghost's fingers trembled over his keyboard, the blue light of multiple monitors casting shadows under his exhausted eyes. Empty energy drink cans and coffee cups created a graveyard of caffeine around his workstation. He'd been analyzing the neural network data for seventy-two hours straight, lines of code blurring together until they almost seemed to move on their own.

Then he saw it.

"No," he whispered, double-checking his findings. Triple-checking. His hands shook as he pulled up the network logs. "No, no, no... WRAITH!"

She appeared in the doorway instantly, as if she

hadn't been sleeping either. Dark circles shadowed her eyes, her hair unwashed and tangled, wearing the same clothes she'd had on for days. Since Thomas.

"Look," Ghost pointed to his main screen, where a complex diagram of quantum encryption patterns pulsed with artificial life. "When Thomas... when he died, his neural interface was still connected to the network. But instead of a clean disconnect, it created a cascade error. A fracture in their quantum encryption."

He pulled up another window, showing lines of base code. "See these patterns? The network operates on a quantum-entangled state. Every connected mind is part of a larger consciousness. When Thomas died fighting the control..."

"The network felt it," Wraith finished, her voice hollow. "Every connected mind felt my brother die."

"And that shared trauma created micro-fractures in their encryption. Like... like cracks in a mirror." Ghost's voice softened. "Thomas's last gift to us."

Mark entered, immediately tensing at the energy in the room. "What's happening?"

"We can break the network," Wraith's voice carried a dangerous edge. "Through my brother's death."

"There's a catch," Ghost continued quickly. "These fractures, they're not enough on their own. We need direct access to their primary servers - the ones in TechNova's headquarters. The most secure building in the city." He pulled up building schematics. "The server room is here, sub-level three. Quantum-shielded, air-gapped from external networks. We'd need to physically connect to upload the exploit."

"When do we leave?" Wraith was already moving toward their weapons cache.

"Wraith, wait," Mark stepped in front of her. "We need to plan this. Think it through."

"I'm done thinking," she snapped, checking the magazine in her pistol. "Every second we wait is another second they're trapped. Like Thomas was trapped."

"And if we rush in and die, what then?" Mark pressed. "Who saves them?"

"Mark's right," Ghost stood, swaying slightly from exhaustion. "The security systems alone will take hours to map. They've upgraded everything since our last intel. New quantum scanners, biometric locks, neural pattern recognition..."

"No." Wraith's voice could have frozen fire. "We go now. Thomas is still in their system. Still part of their network. Every minute we wait is another minute they use his death to control others. I won't..." her voice finally cracked. "I won't let them use my brother like that. Not anymore."

They stared at her, seeing the dangerous edge she'd been walking since Thomas's death. The way grief had crystallized into something sharp and deadly.

"Four hours," Mark offered. "Give us four hours to prep. Please."

She checked her watch. "Three. Then we move."

The next three hours moved with feverish intensity. Ghost's workspace became a hurricane of screens and cables as he prepared their digital arsenal. His fingers flew across keyboards, muttering in mixed English and Mandarin as he coded their exploit.

"The fractures in their encryption," he explained, pulling up complex diagrams, "they appear at regular intervals. Every time the network syncs - which happens every six hours. But Thomas's neural signature..." He zoomed in on a particular pattern. "It's like an echo. Every sync, every connected mind remembers his death for a fraction of a second."

Mark laid out their tactical gear on a makeshift planning table. "How long will we have once we're inside?"

"Four minutes to reach the server room. Two minutes to upload the exploit. After that..." Ghost swallowed hard. "After that, every Project Harmony subject in the building will experience temporary neural disruption. Including the security teams."

"They'll feel what Thomas felt," Wraith said

quietly, checking her weapons with mechanical precision. "Good."

The plan was precise, born of desperation and exhaustion. Ghost had identified a maintenance access through the building's old pneumatic mail system - a relic from before digital transformation. Mark would lead, using his father's training to handle any physical security. Ghost would manage their technical penetration from a mobile setup. And Wraith... Wraith would be their failsafe.

"Remember," Mark stressed as they geared up, "we go in quiet. Get to the server room, upload the exploit, get out. No deviations."

Wraith didn't respond, focusing instead on loading her spare magazines.

The approach to TechNova's headquarters felt surreal in the pre-dawn darkness. The building loomed above them, its glass facade reflecting the city's neon glow. Ghost's tablets showed guard rotations, security sweeps, camera coverage - a digital dance they'd have to navigate perfectly.

"First checkpoint," Ghost whispered through their comms. "Mark, you've got thirty seconds while I loop the cameras."

Mark moved like a shadow, his mother's training guiding each step as he bypassed the external sensors. The maintenance entrance was exactly where Ghost's plans showed - a small panel near ground level, hidden behind decorative landscaping.

"We're in," Mark confirmed as they slipped inside. "Ghost?"

"Working on internal security. These quantum scanners... they're looking for neural patterns. Any Project Harmony subject would be recognized instantly." His fingers danced across his tablet. "Okay, got it looped. Move."

They descended through service corridors, the air growing cooler as they went deeper. Sub-level one passed without incident. Sub-level two required Ghost to hack a biometric lock, sweat beading on his forehead as he raced against security protocols.

Then they reached sub-level three.

"Something's wrong," Mark whispered, holding up his fist for them to stop. "Ghost?"

"I see it. Guard patterns are off. They've doubled security on this level but..." Ghost's voice trailed off as he checked his tablets. "I don't see any alerts. Why would they..."

"Because they're expecting us," Wraith finished. "They knew we'd figure it out eventually."

The server room door loomed ahead, heavy steel reinforced with quantum shielding. Ghost connected his equipment, muttering under his breath as he worked.

"Two minutes to crack the lock," he reported. "Then four minutes inside before the next security sweep. Mark, watch our six. Wraith..."

But Wraith was gone.

"No," Ghost's voice cracked with panic. "No, no, no. Her tracker... she's heading up. Toward the executive floors."

Mark's blood ran cold. "Stay here. Complete the upload. I'll get her."

He moved through the building like a ghost himself, following the signal from Wraith's tracker. His heart pounded with each floor he climbed, knowing every second increased their risk of discovery.

He found her in Roth's office, methodically destroying everything in sight. Family photos shattered on the floor, awards crushed under her boots, desk drawers emptied and scattered.

"Wraith-"

"He kept trophies," her voice was terrifyingly calm as she held up a small box. Inside were neural interface chips, each labeled with a subject number. "Thomas was 23-B. He kept my brother's pain as a paperweight."

She pulled out something else - a small explosive device. Military grade.

"When did you..."

"Does it matter?" Her thumb hovered over the detonator. "They took Thomas. They take everyone. No more."

"Alex," Mark used her real name, stepping

closer. His father's training screamed at him to disarm her, but he knew force wasn't the answer. Not with her. Not after Thomas. "Think about what you're doing."

"I have thought about it. For every second since they put a bullet in my brother's head while I watched." Her voice shook, but her hand remained steady on the detonator. "Did you know they recorded it? His death? I found the file in Roth's computer. They show it to other subjects as a lesson."

Mark's earpiece crackled. "Exploit uploaded," Ghost reported, his voice tense. "But we've got movement. Multiple security teams converging on your position. And... shit. Rodriguez is in the building."

Wraith's laugh was hollow. "Perfect. Let him come. Let him see what happens when you turn someone's brother into a teaching tool."

"This isn't what Thomas died for," Mark took another careful step forward. "You know that. He chose to die rather than let them use him to hurt others. What you're about to do..."

"Don't," she snarled. "Don't you dare use his choice against me. I let them kill him. I chose this mission over my brother's life. So don't tell me what he would have wanted."

"Guys," Ghost's voice was urgent now. "Rodriguez is heading up. Thirty seconds to your position. And... something's wrong with the security teams. Their movements are too coordinated, too precise. I think... I think they're all Project Harmony subjects."

Mark saw the change in Wraith's eyes at those words. Saw her finger tighten on the detonator.

"If I trigger this," she whispered, "it'll overload their neural interfaces. Kill them instantly. Free them, like Thomas is free."

"That's not freedom," Mark kept his voice gentle. "That's revenge. And you're better than that. Thomas believed you were better than that."

"Stop saying his name!" The scream tore from her throat, raw and primal. "You don't get to use him against me! None of you understand what it's like to choose! To watch your little brother forgive you for letting him die!"

Footsteps in the hallway now. Running feet, perfect synchronization.

"Alex," Mark made his choice, stepping directly in front of her. "Pull that trigger, you kill me too. And Ghost. And every innocent person in this building. Is that what you want? More death? More families destroyed?"

Her hand shook. "I have to... I have to make it mean something..."

"It already means something. The exploit worked. We can free them now, Alex. Really free them. Let them live."

The footsteps were right outside now. Any second, Rodriguez would enter.

"Ghost," Mark said quietly, "Execute Protocol Echo. Now."

The lights went out. In the darkness, he heard Wraith's sharp intake of breath as he gently took the detonator from her trembling fingers.

"Run," he whispered, taking her hand. "Like

your brother taught you to live."

They moved through darkness, Ghost guiding them through their earpieces. Behind them, they heard Rodriguez's voice, cold with fury, ordering his teams to search. But they were already gone, sliding through maintenance shafts, emerging into the pre-dawn air.

The safe house was silent when they returned. Ghost took one look at Wraith's face and pulled her into a fierce hug. She stood rigid for a moment, then collapsed against him, broken sounds escaping her throat.

"I'm sorry," she gasped between sobs. "I'm sorry, I almost... I couldn't..."

"Shh," Ghost held her tighter. "We've got you. We're not letting go."

Mark watched them, his own eyes burning. On Ghost's screens, he could see the exploit working - tiny fractures in TechNova's perfect system, spreading like cracks in ice. Thomas's final gift, turning their weapon of control into a path to freedom.

Tomorrow, they would begin the real work. Would start freeing minds, one by one. Would dismantle TechNova's empire of enslaved souls.

But tonight, they held each other as Wraith finally let herself break. Let herself feel the full weight of her brother's sacrifice. Let herself be human again.

Because tomorrow, grief would become purpose.

And TechNova would learn what real freedom meant.

8

The church stood silent in the pre-dawn darkness, its Gothic architecture a shadow against the lightening sky. None of them were particularly religious - their faiths had been tested too many times by the horrors they'd witnessed. But something drew them here, in the quiet hours before their first attempt to free Project Harmony's victims.

Mark entered first, his footsteps echoing in the empty nave. The scent of incense and old wood brought back memories of his mother - not praying, but sitting in churches like this one, teaching him about sanctuary. "Sacred spaces," she'd said, "are powerful not because of any god, but because they hold the weight of human hope and suffering."

Ghost followed, his usual quips dying on his lips as he looked up at the stained glass windows. In the dim light, they were more shadow than color, like the memories of his students that haunted his dreams. He hadn't been in a church since their funerals - Maria, Andy, Kai. Had lit candles for them, not believing in heaven but desperately hoping they'd found peace somewhere.

Wraith entered last, Thomas's bloody graduation photo clutched in her hand. She'd been here before, in the days after his death, screaming at an empty altar until her voice gave out. Now she moved silently, like a ghost herself, toward the banks of votive candles.

They separated naturally, each drawn to different corners of the sacred space, each carrying their own burdens.

Mark's Prayer :

He knelt in a pew near the front, his mother's

gun a heavy weight against his ribs. The wooden beads of his father's old rosary clicked softly between his fingers - not in prayer, but in the same rhythm his dad had used to count breaths during meditation.

"I don't know if you're listening," he whispered to the shadows. "Mom believed. Dad... Dad said belief was less important than action. But I need..." His voice caught. "I need to know we're doing the right thing. That the price we're paying - that Wraith paid with Thomas, that Ghost paid with his students - that it means something."

His eyes burned as he remembered Emily in her hospital bed, Thomas's final smile, the empty eyes of Project Harmony's victims. "Give me strength," he breathed. "Not to fight. I know how to fight. Give me strength to carry them. To be what they need when this gets darker. Because it will get darker, won't it? Before any light comes."

Ghost's Confession:

He stood before the altar, hands shoved in his pockets, shoulders hunched like a guilty child.

Lines of code still ran through his mind, but here they seemed to take on new meaning - strings of ones and zeros becoming questions of existence.

"I taught them to think," he said softly, tears sliding down his cheeks. "To question. To seek truth in patterns. And that's why they were chosen, wasn't it? Because I made them too bright, too curious." He pulled out his phone, displaying a photo of his coding class. Young faces smiled back, unaware of their fate. "Maria loved puzzles. Andy wanted to make games that helped people learn. Kai... Kai just wanted to make his mom proud."

His legs gave out and he sat heavily on the altar steps. "I couldn't save them. My code wasn't good enough, wasn't fast enough. And now I'm using Thomas's death - using his pain - to try to free them. Is that redemption or just another sin?"

Wraith's Lament:

She lit a candle with trembling hands, setting Thomas's photo beside it. In the flickering light, he smiled eternally - frozen in that moment of triumph, before TechNova, before Project Harmony, before she chose the greater good over her brother's life.

"You would understand," she whispered, touching his face in the photo. "You always understood everything. Even at the end, you..." Her voice broke. "You smiled at me. Forgave me. How do I forgive myself?"

The candle flame wavered, casting dancing shadows on Thomas's face. "I'm going to free them, little brother. Every mind they've enslaved. Every soul they've tried to break. But I'm so afraid..." She pressed her forehead against the cool stone of the altar. "I'm afraid of what I'll become doing it. Of the rage inside me. You were always the better one, the kinder one. How do I do this without losing myself?"

They came together naturally, drawn by shared pain and purpose, meeting before the great stained glass window. Dawn was breaking now, sending shafts of colored light through the ancient glass, painting them in fragments of divine fire.

Mark reached for their hands, forming a circle. Ghost's fingers trembled with exhaustion and guilt. Wraith's were cold as ice. But together, they held on.

Above them, worked in glass and lead, were words from the Book of Isaiah:

"Then I heard the voice of the Lord saying, 'Whom shall I send? And who will go for us?' And I said, 'Here am I. Send me.'"

The verse seemed to echo in the empty church, speaking to each of them differently.

To Mark: A calling to lead, to protect, to carry others through darkness.

To Ghost: A chance for redemption, to use his skills to free rather than inadvertently condemn.

To Wraith: A purpose beyond grief, a way to honor Thomas's sacrifice.

"We should go," Ghost finally whispered, his voice rough. "The first extraction team will be ready soon."

"One minute more," Wraith's voice was barely audible. "Just... one more minute."

They stood in silence, holding each other up, letting the colored light wash over them. Each lost in their own prayers, their own hopes, their own fears. But together. Always together.

Because tomorrow they would begin freeing minds from Project Harmony's control. Would face whatever darkness TechNova threw at them. Would probably lose more, suffer more, bleed more.

But here, in this moment, in this sacred space, they found something they desperately needed:

Peace. Purpose. And most importantly, each other.

Mark squeezed their hands once before letting go. "Ready?"

Ghost wiped his eyes, managing a weak smile. "Ready to raise some holy hell."

Wraith touched Thomas's photo one last time, then straightened her spine. "Ready to set them free."

They walked out together into the dawn, carrying a piece of that sacred silence with them.

Behind them, Thomas's candle flickered in a sudden draft, as if waving goodbye. Or perhaps blessing their mission.

The war for humanity's free will was about to begin.

But first, they had needed this moment. This breath. This prayer.

This reminder of what they were really fighting for.

9

The pre-dawn air carried a metallic taste, like blood or circuitry. Mark and Wraith moved through shadows cast by TechNova's tower, each step bringing them closer to either humanity's liberation or their own destruction. In their ears, Ghost's breathing mixed with the soft hum of his equipment.

"First firewall is down," Ghost reported from his mobile command center. "Creating quantum encryption fractures... now."

On his screens, the neural network map pulsed with artificial life. Each light represented a connected mind - thousands of them, all trapped in TechNova's false harmony. He began his attack, using Thomas's neural signature to create tiny cracks in their perfect system.

"Security teams are responding exactly as predicted," he continued, fingers dancing across three keyboards. "They're diverting resources to patch the fractures. Mark, Wraith - you've got four minutes to reach the maintenance access."

Mark led them to the hidden entrance, his mother's training guiding each silent step. The pneumatic mail system access panel yielded to Wraith's tools, revealing the dark passage beyond.

"Wait," Ghost's voice suddenly tensed. "Movement in the tunnel. Neural pattern detected. It's... oh god."

A small figure emerged from the darkness. Maria Chen, thirteen forever, her face serene and empty. "Hello, Teacher," she said in that horrible mechanical voice. "We've been expecting you."

Ghost's hands froze over his keyboards, his breath catching. "Maria..."

"Your attempts to disrupt harmony are inefficient," she continued, head tilting at an unnatural angle. "Submit to integration, and the pain will be minimal."

"Ghost," Mark said quietly, "stay with us. She's not-"

"I know," Ghost's voice cracked. "I know she's not really Maria anymore. But..." His fingers resumed typing, faster now. "But maybe she can be again. Wraith?"

Wraith was already moving, neural disruptor raised. "I'm sorry," she whispered, and fired.

Maria's body crumpled, the neural interface temporarily overloaded. Mark caught her before she hit the ground, laying her gently aside.

"She'll wake up when we upload the exploit," Wraith assured Ghost. "She'll have the same choice as everyone else."

They continued deeper, descending through maintenance shafts toward sub-level five. The air grew colder, heavy with the hum of quantum processors.

"Security teams are adapting to the fractures faster than expected," Ghost reported, his voice professional again despite the encounter with Maria. "They're using some kind of quantum machine learning. The network is... evolving."

"Can you counter it?" Mark asked, checking another corner.

"Not directly. But maybe..." Ghost's typing speed increased. "If I use Thomas's signature as a quantum key, route it through the fracture points... yes. Creating cascading disruptions now."

The lights flickered above them. Somewhere, an alarm began to wail.

"Multiple neural patterns converging on your position," Ghost warned. "They're using the network to coordinate. Moving like a hive mind."

They reached a security checkpoint. Through the reinforced glass, they could see Project Harmony subjects manning the stations - men and women moving with perfect, inhuman synchronization.

"Remember," Mark said quietly, "they're all victims. We disable, don't kill."

Wraith nodded grimly, checking her neural

disruptor's charge. "Ghost, ready?"

"Initiating checkpoint systems crash in three... two... one..."

The security stations went dark. Mark and Wraith moved with practiced efficiency, neural disruptors dropping the controlled subjects before they could raise alarm.

"Jesus," Mark breathed, seeing their faces up close. Young, old, every ethnicity - all wearing that same empty serenity. "How many people have they taken?"

"Too many," Wraith's voice was steel. "But not for much longer."

They reached the quantum shielding protecting sub-level five. Ghost's voice crackled with increasing static as the shielding interfered with their comms.

"The hub's quantum encryption is adapting to my attacks," he reported. "They're... they're using Thomas's neural pattern against us. Turning it into a weapon."

"What?" Wraith's hands stilled on her

equipment.

"The network, it's learning. Taking Thomas's resistance and... and using it to strengthen their control. We need to move faster."

Mark began setting charges on the shielding. "How long until-"

"Company!" Ghost's warning came just as the elevator doors opened.

Rodriguez stepped out, flanked by more Project Harmony subjects. But these were different - their movements more fluid, more natural. More dangerous.

"Improved models," Rodriguez smiled coldly. "Using your brother's neural pattern, Dr. Kane. His resistance taught us so much about strengthening our control."

The quantum processing hub was a cathedral of technology, its crystalline structure rising thirty feet into the sub-level's cavernous space. Cooling systems hummed a complex harmony, maintaining the precise temperature needed for quantum operations. The air itself seemed to vibrate with computational power, carrying the weight of thousands of enslaved minds.

Rodriguez stood at its center, surrounded by his elite Project Harmony subjects - twenty men and women chosen for their exceptional neural compatibility. Their movements were unsettling in their perfection, each step precisely synchronized as they encircled Mark and Wraith. The subjects' neural interfaces glowed with a faint blue light beneath their skin, pulsing in unified rhythm.

"Beautiful, isn't it?" Rodriguez's voice carried the fervor of a true believer. He gestured to his perfect soldiers, their blank faces serene. "Look at them. Really look. No doubt clouding their thoughts. No fear holding them back. No chaos disrupting their purpose. This is what humanity could be - what it should be."

Through their comms, Ghost's fingers created a steady rhythm of keystrokes. Multiple screens surrounded him in his mobile command center, each displaying different aspects of the network's quantum architecture.

"Upload at sixty percent," he reported, his voice tense with concentration. "The neural network is... wait. Something's happening. The quantum patterns are shifting. It's like... like they're remembering how to be random."

The first changes were subtle, almost imperceptible. Sarah Chen, one of Rodriguez's elite soldiers, twitched her left hand - a tiny movement, but one that broke her perfect synchronization. Next to her, Michael Patel's rigid posture softened by a fraction of a degree. Their eyes, once empty mirrors, began showing the first ripples of confusion.

"What are you doing?" Rodriguez's composure cracked as he noticed these minute rebellions. He pulled out his neural control tablet, its holographic display showing thousands of neural patterns beginning to fluctuate. "Security override alpha! Resume standard protocols!"

The tablet's screen filled with warning messages:

QUANTUM SYNC ERROR

NEURAL PATTERN DEVIATION DETECTED

CONSCIOUSNESS CORRUPTION WARNING

"They can't hear you anymore," Wraith's voice was quiet, deadly. Her hand touched the pocket holding Thomas's photo. "Not really. They're hearing him now. Feeling what he felt. Every moment of clarity, every surge of defiance, every beat of his heart as he chose humanity over harmony."

"Impossible." Rodriguez's fingers flew over the tablet's controls. "These subjects are enhanced using your brother's own resistance patterns. We turned his defiance into a weapon, used it to strengthen our control. They can't possibly-"

He was cut off by a sound that made Mark's combat-trained muscles tense - laughter. Sarah Chen, her neural interface flickering erratically, was laughing. Not the empty chuckle of Project Harmony subjects, but real, human laughter that carried years of suppressed pain and joy.

"Upload at seventy-five percent," Ghost reported, his voice thick with emotion. "The neural patterns... they're not just changing. They're remembering. Every connected mind is experiencing Thomas's final moments. His clarity. His choice. His... his humanity."

The hub's crystalline structure began pulsing with new colors, quantum states shifting as thousands of minds started waking up. The air filled with the scent of ozone as cooling systems struggled to manage the increased neural activity.

Rodriguez's fingers trembled as he input override codes, each failure causing the tablet's warnings to flash more urgently:

QUANTUM COHERENCE FAILING

NEURAL SYNC DEGRADING

INDIVIDUAL CONSCIOUSNESS PATTERNS EMERGING

WARNING: CASCADE FAILURE IMMINENT

"Security teams to sub-level five!" His voice cracked with desperation. "Full containment protocols! Neural suppression authorized! I need-"

"Look at your screens," Mark interrupted, his tactical training noting every micro-expression of fear crossing Rodriguez's face. "Look at what's really happening to your perfect network."

The hub's main display showed neural patterns like a living constellation - thousands of points of light that had once moved in perfect synchronization. Now those lights were breaking formation, each finding its own rhythm. Some clustered in natural groups, others pulsed in solitude, all moving to music only they could hear.

"Eighty percent," Ghost's voice shook with triumph and tears. "Maria... oh god, Maria's neural patterns are stabilizing. She's remembering how to code. Her mind is actually rewriting the network's base protocols as she wakes up."

The elite soldiers were fully breaking down now. Sarah Chen fell to her knees, her neural interface flickering wildly as tears streamed down her face. "I remember," she whispered, her voice hoarse from years of disuse. "I remember everything. My daughter's birthday. My husband's laugh. The feeling of rain..."

Michael Patel stood perfectly still, but his eyes -

his real, human eyes - filled with tears as decades of suppressed emotions crashed through his consciousness. "What have we done?" he breathed. "What did we let them do to us?"

"No," Rodriguez backed away, his gun shaking as he aimed it first at Mark, then Wraith, then his awakening soldiers. "No, no, NO! Security override beta! Neural purge authorization: HARMONY-PRIME!"

The hub's crystals pulsed red with the purge command, but something else happened - something impossible. The neural interfaces, instead of terminating their hosts, began broadcasting Thomas's final moments to every connected mind:

Thomas, fighting through the control to smile at his sister.

Thomas, choosing death over submission.

Thomas, showing them all that humanity was worth any price.

"Ninety percent," Ghost reported, his voice carrying wonder. "The quantum encryption... it's not just breaking down. It's evolving. Transforming into something new. Something chosen."

Through their neural interfaces, the awakening subjects began sharing their own memories:

Sarah Chen remembered her daughter's first steps.

Michael Patel recalled the poem he'd written for his wife.

Maria, in her coding class, felt the joy of creation again.

Each memory, each emotion, each choice rippled through the network, strengthening the fractures in TechNova's perfect harmony.

"You don't understand what you're destroying!" Rodriguez screamed, firing wildly. Bullets pinged off the hub's crystalline structure, sending rainbow refractions dancing across walls that had only known sterile white. "We gave them peace! We took away their pain, their doubt, their fear!"

"You took away their humanity," Wraith's voice carried the weight of Thomas's sacrifice. "Their right to feel pain, to know doubt, to face fear. Their right to choose."

The hub's displays showed scenes from across the city:

In TechNova's lobby:

Rebecca Martinez, receptionist and Project Harmony Subject 42-A, stopped mid-greeting. Her practiced smile faltered, then transformed into something real as tears began falling. She reached up, touching her face, feeling her own expressions for the first time in years.

In the rehabilitation centers:

James Wilson, Subject 15-C, ripped off his neural dampener. Pain flooded his consciousness - real, human pain - and he laughed through his tears. "I feel," he kept saying. "I feel, I feel, I feel!"

In corporate offices:

Executive boardrooms erupted in chaos as controlled minds broke free. Some collapsed, overwhelmed by returning memories. Others stood, shaking with rage at what had been done to them. All of them, finally, choosing their own reactions.

"Ninety-five percent," Ghost's voice cracked with emotion. "Neural patterns are... they're forming new connections. Voluntary ones. Like a massive social network, but made of pure consciousness. They're choosing who to connect with, how to share memories, what to feel..."

The hub's crystalline structure blazed with new colors as thousands of minds discovered free will again. Each neural interface pulsed with individual rhythm, creating a symphony of human consciousness that made Project Harmony's forced synchronization look pale and lifeless in comparison.

Rodriguez staggered, his gun hand shaking violently as he watched his life's work transform. On his tablet, warning messages cascaded:

QUANTUM COHERENCE CRITICAL

NEURAL OVERRIDE PROTOCOLS FAILING

CONSCIOUSNESS INTEGRATION: ERROR

WARNING: INDIVIDUAL CHOICE PATTERNS DETECTED

SYSTEM TRANSFORMATION IMMINENT

"You don't understand," he whispered, his composure finally shattering completely. "I saw what freedom did to us. The wars, the hatred, the endless suffering. I watched my own family tear itself apart with bad choices, with freedom used wrongly. Project Harmony was meant to save us from ourselves!"

Through their comms, Ghost's typing suddenly stopped. "Mark, Wraith... you need to see this. The network, it's showing us memories. His memories."

The hub's displays flickered, showing fragments of Rodriguez's past:

- A young boy watching his parents' violent arguments

- A teenager discovering his sister's drug addiction

- A man watching society tear itself apart with conflict

- The first Project Harmony tests, promising peace through control

"You think you were helping them?" Wraith's voice carried dangerous quiet. "Look at what you really did. Look at them."

The elite soldiers were fully awake now, their faces showing the full spectrum of human emotion. Sarah Chen held herself, rocking slightly as she processed years of lost time. Michael Patel stared at his hands, remembering all the things they had done under control.

"Upload complete," Ghost announced softly. "Thomas's choice has reached every connected mind. But there's something else happening. The network... it's not just breaking. It's healing. Differently for each mind."

The displays showed the process:

- Some minds chose to maintain certain connections, finding strength in voluntary unity

- Others chose complete independence, relishing their restored individuality

- Many formed small, organic groups, sharing memories and support

- Each consciousness finding its own path back

to humanity

"Maria's doing something remarkable," Ghost continued, awe in his voice. "She's writing new code, creating safe spaces in the network for recovering minds. Support groups formed of pure consciousness. She remembers everything I taught her about ethical programming, and she's using it to help others heal."

Rodriguez fired again, his shot going wild as his perfect soldiers stepped away from him. "Stop this! You have no idea what chaos you're unleashing! The pain they'll have to feel again, the choices they'll have to face!"

"That's exactly what we're giving back to them," Mark advanced steadily. "The right to feel pain. The right to make mistakes. The right to be human."

The hub room was filling now with awakened subjects, drawn by the quantum echoes of consciousness being reborn. Their faces showed everything Rodriguez had tried to erase - fear, anger, confusion, hope, joy, sorrow... humanity in all its messy glory.

"The neural network is stabilizing," Ghost reported. "But it's fundamentally transformed. The quantum encryption only works through conscious choice now. No forced connections, no override protocols. It's becoming something new. Something..."

"Something Thomas would have been proud of," Wraith finished, tears streaming down her face. "A way for minds to connect by choice, to share and heal and grow together. Not harmony through control, but harmony through freedom."

Rodriguez's gun clattered to the floor as he fell to his knees. Around him, his perfect world was becoming something he couldn't control, couldn't predict, couldn't force into his vision of peace.

The elevator doors opened with a soft chime that seemed obscenely normal given the chaos unfolding. Maxwell Roth stepped out, his expensive suit immaculate, his silver hair perfectly styled. But his eyes - his eyes held something close to madness as he surveyed his crumbling empire.

"Fascinating," he said, his cultured voice carrying through the hub room. "Truly fascinating. Rodriguez, my old friend, it seems your perfect system had a fatal flaw. It never accounted for the sheer... stubbornness of human consciousness."

Rodriguez looked up at his boss, his mentor, the man who had funded Project Harmony from its inception. "Sir, I can still contain this. If we initiate a full neural purge-"

"You'd kill them all," Roth cut him off, walking casually through the crowd of awakening subjects. "And what would that prove? That we can only achieve perfect harmony through death?" He laughed softly. "No, I think it's time we witnessed what we've really created here."

The hub's displays showed neural patterns continuing to shift and evolve:

QUANTUM NETWORK STATUS:

- Individual Consciousness Patterns: 15,742 and rising

- Voluntary Neural Connections: 3,891 and rising

\- Forced Sync Protocols: OFFLINE

\- New Code Integration: IN PROGRESS

"Sir," Ghost's voice carried disbelief through their comms. "The network... Roth's neural signature. He's not... he was never..."

"Connected?" Roth smiled, tapping his temple. "Of course not. Did you think I would submit my own consciousness to such control? I am an architect, not a subject. I wanted to see what humanity would become under perfect control. And now," he spread his arms, indicating the chaos around them, "I get to see what happens when that control breaks."

Wraith stepped forward, her hand going to her weapon. "You watched. All this time, you just watched. When they took Thomas, when they broke all these people..."

"I observed," Roth corrected. "Scientifically. Dispassionately. Human consciousness is such a fascinating thing. The way it fights, the way it breaks, the way it... adapts." He turned to one of the awakening subjects. "Tell me, my dear, how does it feel to be truly conscious again?"

Sarah Chen met his gaze, her restored humanity allowing her to show the full force of her hatred. "We remember everything," she said, her voice shaking. "Everything you made us do. Everything you took from us."

"Perfect," Roth's smile widened. "Simply perfect. The raw emotion, the pure human response. So much more interesting than the artificial harmony we imposed."

"You're insane," Mark realized, his father's training screaming at him to eliminate the threat Roth represented.

"Insane? I gave humanity what it always claimed to want - peace, unity, purpose. And now your brother," he nodded to Wraith, "has shown them something far more intriguing. The power of conscious choice. The strength of willing sacrifice. The beauty of... chaos."

Through their comms, Ghost's voice was urgent. "The network is showing something else. Roth's private servers, his personal research. My God...

Project Harmony was never meant to be permanent. It was an experiment. He wanted to see what would happen when humanity regained consciousness after years of control."

"A grand experiment in human nature," Roth confirmed, seemingly unconcerned by the horrified faces around him. "And the results are fascinating. Look how they form new connections, how they process their trauma, how they choose to rebuild their consciousness. Such valuable data."

The hub's crystals pulsed with the rage of awakening minds as they processed this revelation. Their years of enslavement had been nothing but research notes to this man.

"Maria's found something else," Ghost reported, his voice shaking with anger. "Contingency protocols. If the experiment failed, if the subjects couldn't be controlled... there's a quantum failsafe. A way to... to..."

"To end the experiment cleanly," Roth finished, pulling out a small device. "After all, what's the point of an experiment if you can't control all the variables? Including termination?"

The room froze. Even the newly awakened subjects felt the weight of the threat through their neural interfaces.

"Don't," Wraith's voice carried the same tone it had when she chose to let Thomas die. "Don't you dare try to take their choice away again."

"My dear Dr. Kane," Roth's smile never wavered, "I'm giving them the ultimate choice. Freedom... or oblivion. Isn't that what your brother chose? What you chose for him?"

Roth never saw Mark move. Years of his father's training, of learning to strike when the enemy was focused on their own voice, paid off in one fluid motion. The quantum failsafe device clattered across the floor as Roth fell, his perfect composure finally broken.

"Fascinating," he managed to say one last time, before Sarah Chen and the other awakened subjects surrounded him, their restored humanity showing in their eyes as they took control of their former captor.

The aftermath was a blur of authorities, of awakened minds helping each other cope, of a new kind of order emerging from the chaos. But finally, as dawn broke over the city, Mark, Ghost, and Wraith found themselves alone in the church where they'd prayed just days before.

The morning light filtered through the stained glass, painting them in fragments of color. They sat in the front pew, exhausted, triumphant, broken, and healing - just like the minds they'd helped free.

"Maria's organizing support groups," Ghost said softly, breaking the sacred silence. "Using the transformed network to help people recover their memories, process their trauma. She remembers everything about coding, about teaching others. But she also remembers... remembers being trapped. Says it's like watching yourself sleepwalk through years of your life."

Wraith leaned against him, her brother's photo held loosely in her hands. "Thomas would have loved seeing how the network changed. How it became something that helps instead of controls. He always said technology should serve humanity, not the other way around."

Mark watched the candles they'd lit - one for Thomas, one for Ghost's students, one for every mind they'd helped free. "My parents spent years preparing me for a war they never got to fight. But I think... I think they'd be proud of this war we did fight. Not with guns or fists, but with choice. With humanity."

They sat in comfortable silence for a moment, letting the weight of everything settle around them. Then Ghost pulled out his tablet, showing them the transformed neural network - thousands of points of light, each moving to its own rhythm but forming something beautiful in their freedom.

"We should probably run," he said practically. "TechNova's gone, but there will be others. People who want to control, to force harmony."

"Let them come," Wraith's voice carried new strength. "We'll be ready. All of us. Every free mind choosing to stand together."

Mark smiled, remembering his mother's words: "The strongest weapons are the ones you can't see. Like hope. Like choice. Like love."

They stood together, their shadows mixing with the colored light from the windows. Outside, the city was awakening to true freedom, to real choice, to genuine harmony born of individual will.

But in here, in this moment, they were just three broken people who had somehow helped heal the world.

Three fighters who had won not through force, but through faith in humanity's power to choose.

Three friends who had become family in the crucible of their mission.

Ghost touched the neural network display one last time, showing them the beautiful chaos of free consciousness. Wraith held her brother's photo to her heart, feeling his choice echo in every liberated mind. And Mark... Mark finally understood what his parents had trained him for - not just to fight, but to protect the fundamental right that made humans human:

The right to choose.

The right to feel.

The right to be gloriously, chaotically, perfectly imperfect.

Together, they walked out into the morning light, ready for whatever came next.

Because some wars end not with victory or defeat, but with transformation.

And some families are forged not in blood, but in the fire of fighting for what's right.

Together, this family drew back the curtain of control, and allowed the sun to shine on a free world once again.

Epilogue

15 years later

The Rivera family cabin looked much the same as it had during Mark's childhood training sessions, though now children's toys mingled with the survival gear, and family photos covered walls that once held tactical maps. Outside, the Colorado mountains caught the setting sun, painting the snow in shades of gold and purple.

Ten-year-old Thomas Kane Rivera - named for the uncle he'd never met - sat cross-legged on the floor, his younger sister Sarah perched on the couch behind him. Their eyes were wide as they listened to their Uncle Mark's story, a tale they'd begged to hear countless times before.

"But how did you know the neural network would transform instead of just breaking?" Thomas asked, his quick mind - so like his namesake's - always seeking technical details. "When you uploaded the exploit..."

Mark smiled, remembering Ghost's frantic coding sessions. "We didn't know for sure. But your Uncle Ghost - he understood something about consciousness that TechNova never did. That real connections, real harmony, can only come from choice."

"Tell them about Maria again," Sarah piped up. At eight years old, she was fascinated by the young coder who had helped rebuild the network into something healing rather than controlling.

"Maria Chen," Mark's voice softened with memory. "She runs the biggest neural recovery program now. Uses the transformed network to help people process their trauma, rebuild their sense of self. Ghost says she's a better teacher than he ever was."

"Is that why Aunt Wraith named her research center after Uncle Thomas?" Thomas asked. "Because he showed people how to choose?"

Mark nodded, glancing at the photo on the mantle - Thomas's graduation picture, no longer bloody but carefully restored, watching over the family he'd helped save.

"The Thomas Kane Center for Neural Ethics," he confirmed. "Your Aunt Wraith... she turned her grief into something powerful. The center makes sure no one can ever use neural technology to control minds again. They develop new ways to help consciousness heal, grow, connect - but always by choice. Never by force."

Sarah hugged her knees to her chest. "Were you scared? When you were fighting TechNova?"

Mark considered the question carefully. "Yes," he admitted. "But your grandparents taught me something important about fear. It's not about not being afraid. It's about choosing to act anyway, when something matters enough."

"Like family," Thomas said solemnly.

"Exactly like family." Mark reached out to ruffle his nephew's hair. "Speaking of which..."

"Like the night your mom got stabbed," Mark said quietly, watching his sister appear in the doorway. Emily moved with a slight limp now, a permanent reminder of that night, but her eyes were as sharp as ever.

"Are you telling them that story again?" she asked, though her smile was fond. "They'll have nightmares."

"No we won't!" Sarah protested. "Uncle Mark says we're Riveras, and Riveras don't get nightmares. We process and adapt!"

Emily laughed, settling into her favorite armchair. "Oh really? Is that what Uncle Mark says?"

"Tell them how it started, Em," Mark encouraged. "They should hear it from you."

Emily's hand unconsciously touched her side, where the scars still marked her brush with TechNova's enforcers. "I was a journalist," she began, her voice taking on the storytelling cadence she'd perfected over years of sharing this tale. "And I found something I wasn't supposed to find. Files about missing people, about a program called Project Harmony..."

"And then the bad men came," Thomas finished, having heard this part many times. "But you managed to call Uncle Mark!"

"I did," Emily's eyes met her brother's across the room. "Because I knew, no matter what, Mark would come. That's what family means in our world - knowing someone will always come for you, no matter the cost."

"Even if it means fighting an evil corporation?" Sarah asked excitedly.

"Even if it means fighting the whole world," Mark said softly. "I remember that night so clearly. Getting your mom's call, hearing the fear in her voice... Everything changed in that moment. Everything our parents had trained me for suddenly made sense."

"Grandma and Grandpa knew," Thomas said with the certainty of a child who'd grown up with the legend. "That's why they taught you all those things. They knew someone would have to fight the bad guys someday."

Emily's eyes glistened slightly. "They knew something was coming. They just didn't live to see what it was. But they made sure Mark would be ready when it did."

"And then you met Uncle Ghost and Aunt Wraith!" Sarah bounced excitedly. "Tell about how you played games together first!"

Mark laughed. "Brawl Stars. Your Uncle Ghost still claims he carried us through every match, though Aunt Wraith would disagree..."

"But you know what the really amazing part is?" Mark leaned forward, his voice softening. "It wasn't just about stopping the bad guys. It was about what we chose to become afterward. Look at your Uncle Ghost now - teaching ethical coding to kids, making sure technology helps people instead of controlling them."

"And Aunt Wraith's neural research!" Thomas added enthusiastically. "Mom says she's helping people's minds heal, using the same network that used to hurt them."

Emily smiled at her son's excitement. "That's right. And you know why she named you Thomas?"

The boy nodded solemnly. "Because Uncle Thomas showed everyone that choosing to be free is more important than being safe. That's why his picture watches over us," he pointed to the graduation photo on the mantle.

Sarah yawned, fighting to keep her eyes open. "But weren't you scared, Mom? When you got hurt?"

Emily's hand found Mark's, squeezing it gently. "I was terrified, sweetheart. But I knew your Uncle Mark would come. Just like I know he'd come for you, or Thomas, or anyone in our family. That's who he is. That's who our parents trained him to be."

"A hero?" Sarah's eyes were drooping despite her best efforts.

"No," Mark shook his head. "Just a brother. Just

family."

As the children finally drifted off to sleep, Emily and Mark moved to the cabin's back deck. The mountains loomed dark against the star-filled sky, the same view that had watched them train as children.

"They love that story," Emily said softly, leaning against the railing. "Though I notice you leave out some of the darker parts."

"They'll learn those when they're older," Mark watched a satellite trace its way across the stars - one of Ghost's new secure communication network, keeping the transformed neural web safe. "About Thomas's choice. About Maria and the other children. About how close we came to losing everything."

"Do you ever regret it?" Emily asked. "Taking on TechNova, risking everything?"

Mark turned to his sister, really looking at her - the slight limp from her stab wounds, the grey starting to thread through her hair, the strength that had never wavered.

"Never," his voice was firm. "Not for a second. You know what Dad used to say about family?", "That it's the only thing worth dying for?", "No," Mark smiled. "That it's the only thing worth living for. Everything I did - everything we all did - it was about protecting the right to choose our own family. Whether that's by blood, like you and me, or by choice, like Ghost and Wraith."Emily wiped away a tear. "They're going to face their own battles someday, aren't they? Thomas and Sarah?"

"Probably. The world's better now, but not perfect. There will always be people who want to control others, to force their version of harmony." Mark looked back at the cabin, where his niece and nephew slept peacefully. "But they'll be ready. Not just with training, like we were, but with understanding. They know what freedom costs, what it's worth."

"And they'll have you," Emily's voice carried absolute certainty. "Their Uncle Mark, who would burn down the world to keep them safe."

"Not burn it down," Mark corrected gently.

"Transform it. Like Thomas did. Like we all did. That's the real legacy we're leaving them - not just the ability to fight, but the wisdom to know what's worth fighting for."

They stood in comfortable silence, watching the stars wheel overhead. Inside, Thomas and Sarah slept under their uncle's watchful gaze, while on the mantle, another Thomas smiled down at the family his sacrifice had helped create.

Somewhere in the transformed neural network, minds connected and healed by choice, not force. In his coding school, Ghost taught another generation about ethical technology. In her research center, Wraith helped consciousness heal and grow.

And here, in the cabin where it all began, Mark Rivera stood guard over the future - not with weapons or training, but with love. With family. With the unshakeable certainty that some things were worth any price.

Because in the end, that's what his parents had really trained him for. Not just to fight, but to protect. Not just to survive, but to ensure others could thrive. Not just to resist control, but to nurture choice.

"I love you, little sister," he said softly.

Emily leaned her head on his shoulder, just like she had when they were children. "I love you too, big brother. Thank you for always coming when I call."

"Always will," he promised. "That's what family means."

Above them, the stars continued their eternal dance, free and chaotic and perfect in their chosen paths. Just like the minds they'd helped liberate. Just like the family they'd built. Just like the future they protected.

And in that moment, Mark knew with absolute certainty that every choice, every sacrifice, every battle had been worth it. Because it had led here - to peace, to family, to love freely chosen and fiercely protected.

That was the real victory. That was the true harmony.

That was the legacy they'd pass on, generation after generation, in the stories they told and the choices they made.

Because some things were worth fighting for.

Some things were worth dying for.

But family - family was worth living for.

And that was the greatest choice of all.